Robak's Firm

By Joe L. Hensley

Robak's Firm

JOE L. HENSLEY

PUBLISHED FOR THE CRIME CLUB BY
DOUBLEDAY & COMPANY, INC.
GARDEN CITY, NEW YORK
1987

ACKNOWLEDGMENTS

"Tourist," copyright 1984 by Halo Publications, reprinted from *The Saint Magazine*.

"Searcher," copyright 1984 by Halo Publications, reprinted from *The Saint Magazine*.

"Finder," copyright 1984 by Halo Publications, reprinted from *The Saint Magazine*.

"On the Rocks," copyright 1985 by Renown Publications, reprinted from *Mike Shayne Mystery Magazine*.

"The Decision," copyright 1984 by Davis Publications, Inc., reprinted from *Ellery Queen's Mystery Magazine*.

"The Home," copyright 1985 by Davis Publications, Inc., reprinted from *Ellery Queen's Mystery Magazine*.

"Savant," copyright 1985 by Mercury Press Inc., reprinted from *The Magazine of Fantasy & Science Fiction*.

"All That Mattered," copyright 1987 by Josh Pachter and Joe L. Hensley.

"Dog Man," "Judicial Discretion," "The Profession," "The Retiree," "Trial," "Truly Yours, John R. Jacks," and "Whistler," copyright 1987 by Joe L. Hensley.

Library of Congress Cataloging-in-Publication Data

Hensley, Joe L., 1926–
Robak's firm.

I. Title.
PS3558.E55R67 1987   813'.54   86-23929
ISBN 0-385-23829-0

Contents

Robak's Firm

Foreword

Some years ago I put together a collection of my early "suspense" stories and that book was published under the title *Final Doors* by Doubleday, a courteous conglomerate that's also mistakenly published some of my novels. In that collection there were stories that had been published by various magazines, *Alfred Hitchcock's, Rogue, The Magazine of Fantasy & Science Fiction, Swank,* etc., and some that I did for the book itself. There were three collaborations with my good friends Harlan Ellison (2) and Gene DeWeese (1). Those collaborations, it is hoped, lent some credibility to the book and, as such things go, the book sold fairly well.

But the years have rolled on and the one thing you can count on from a writer is that he'll write more until someone forcibly restrains or buries him.

I'm still, as I type this, a circuit court judge and whatever minor gift I have as a writer is still viewed with some alarm by my colleagues of the bench and those members of the bar who practice where I judge. That, roughly, is a twenty-county area in southeast Indiana. They say to me, with false camaraderie, "What's going now on the typewriter, Judge?"

I've learned to shrug and say as little as possible. When I talk too much I see the small, superior smiles on alien faces. The kind of smiles that one observes as people watch monkeys at a zoo. I can't help this legal reaction and so I try to ignore it.

On the other side of it I've several times been asked, by editors and other writers, what someone like me was doing in a field like the suspense field.

To requote an old, tired line: "Just lucky, I guess."

Once, a long time ago, I tried to give up writing on the thought that writing just didn't mix well with being a black-robed judge. That didn't work out well. I found that when I didn't write I got nervous and edgy and wound up telling stories to the neighborhood kids, dogs, and cats. Most of the neighbors didn't mind it for their kids, a tough-minded, resilient crew into Robert Bloch and Stephen King, but complained about the dogs and cats because, after hearing my stories, some of those animals slept poorly and wouldn't go out after dark.

So, by demand of my neighbors if not the reading public, I continue to turn on my computer or sit at my typewriter and practice what's loosely been referred to as my "craft." Some people think I'm good at it (thank you, son Mike and Aunt Peg).

Writing, whatever else it is, also takes a part of you with each story. You've used up something. It can be used again, but not perpetually and not in the same way. What happens inside when something there feeds out onto paper is that you become changed with the bleeding. It isn't that you're any less, it's that you're different. So the years have made me different, I admit it, and I'm unawed by it.

I've made a lot of friends in the business (and probably a few enemies). I won't try to name those friends in this short foreword. It wasn't written to do that. And it wasn't written to say goodbye to those who've gone on to other places in the dark.

This is a foreword, an introduction if you will.

So let me introduce you to Josh Pachter, who collaborated with me on "All That Mattered." Josh is a young teacher employed by the University of Maryland and he works for them now in West Germany. He's also the editor of a number of anthologies and I came upon him because of the anthologies. His publishing connections began in the Netherlands, but now they're pretty much worldwide. He writes short stories for *Ellery Queen's* and other magazines and now is finishing a novel. I like him. Recently, in New York for the mystery writers' meeting, we kicked around town together with some kindred spirits like Al Nussbaum, and Mike Nevins (who is, no kidding, an Edgar winner and a law professor in St. Louis—me being not the only odd duck in the pond).

One of the anthologies Josh put together for his Dutch publisher was a group of collaborations with people like Ed Hoch, K Arne Blom (of Sweden), Jon L. Breen, and me, to mention a few. Josh and I did "All That Mattered" for that. Later the story was sold to *The Saint* but died there when that magazine faded from sight after a few issues. No one else bought it, but Josh liked it, I liked it, and our joint agent on the story, Virginia Kidd, liked it. So here 'tis.

Final Doors, the earlier collection, had some stories in it that were category crossers and so does this book. If you like that sort of thing I'll point out "Truly Yours, John R. Jacks" and "Savant." If you don't like crossovers then you've been warned.

Other than that the stories are just suspense stories about nice people just like your good friends and neighbors.

Sure they are . . .

"Dog Man" was written because I have a younger sister who, when we were kids, could do about anything with animals. I used to stoke furnaces and I can remember paying her part of the money I got to go with me and keep the dogs off. "Decision" came about because I've sometimes decided things rightly for the wrong reasons. "On the Rocks" is the outgrowth of my weekly, three-season golf game with the Jug Hunters. I keep score for them if you begin to try figuring who "Judge Hinshaw" is. Just goes to show how writers can twist things. I am, of course, completely honest in the golf scoring. "Savant" and perhaps "Whistler" happened because I hold hearings at the Madison State Hospital, a place where the mentally ill are treated. "The Home" and "The Profession" and possibly "The Retiree" are what-if stories with legal or judicial backgrounds. Etc.

But I'll let you start with "Tourist," which is one of those stories that happen when you sit down at the typewriter wondering what'll happen next. It's the first of three Cannert stories in the book. The other two are "Searcher" and "Finder." I'm sure you'll like Cannert. I do. A sweet old man . . .

Joe L. Hensley
Madison, Indiana

Tourist

Cannert came upon the motel after still another day of driving. The motel was off the interstate on a secondary road. It wasn't much different from others he'd seen and decided against, except it seemed well kept and was freshly painted.

Martha's last card had come from Lake City, two hundred plus miles away. She liked back roads, clean quiet places, easy driving.

He dug out a map from the cluttered glove compartment of the Ford and unfolded it. He was north of Jax, but still in Florida, and within driving range of Lake City.

Beyond the motel, Cannert could see and smell the ocean. The long, low building was far from new, but it was white-tile-roofed and attractive, the kind of small place Martha would have been drawn to. Cannert counted the units. There were twenty-eight.

There was a sign at the highway entrance. It read "Mom's Motel. Singles $14, Doubles $18." Below, in smaller letters, "Weekly Rates." A small neon vacancy sign glowed.

Martha might have seen the sign if she'd passed this way, Cannert thought. He'd sent her on south to scout for a place months back, while he was still in the hospital. It had been a mistake to let her leave without him. He was almost sure now that she was dead. It was possible she'd just left him, given him up as a futile job, but he didn't believe so.

He parked the Ford in front of the office unit and got slowly out. From the inlet behind the motel there came a sharp, fish smell. White gulls wheeled and flashed over the water.

Two people, a man and a woman, watched him into the office, inspecting him. The man put down his newspaper and Cannert saw the familiar headlines he'd read yesterday in Jacksonville. Two days back and several hundred miles away, near Live Oak, an unknown, possibly demented rifleman had conducted target practice on the office of a motel about the size of this one, killing two, wounding one. Cannert supposed that had made many motel managers suspicious.

"Could I see a room?" he inquired gently.

The man nodded, relaxing a bit. He was a big, fleshy man, not yet old, but not young. He was much larger than Cannert.

"You sure can, sir. You'll find our place clean and respectable. We even have a pool if you like to swim." His voice had a touch of New England in it.

The woman went back to the book she'd been reading. Her eyes had shrewdly estimated Cannert and his probable worth and been unimpressed.

Cannert followed the big man down a well-weeded walk. The motel man's step was light, like that of many heavy men.

The room Cannert was shown was acceptable. Sunlight came through a clean west window. The bedspread was faded but immaculate. The towels in the bath were thinning but still serviceable. There was a quiet window air conditioner.

Cannert nodded his approval and followed the fat man back to the office. "I'll stay a week. Perhaps even longer if the fishing around here's as good as I've heard it is."

"Try the pier near Citadel City, five miles south," the

motel man advised amiably. "Or you can rent a boat in town." He shrugged. "I'm not a fisherman, but I hear it's okay."

Cannert looked out the office window. Only a few other cars were parked in front of units and it was late in the day.

"Looks as if business isn't so good."

The motel man gave him a sharp glance. "We make do all right. Times are hard. This is better than welfare, and lots better than being cold. Took Em and me five years down here to get the damned Maine cold out of our bones." He shook his head. "We'll never go back."

"Is your pool salt or fresh?"

"Salt. Can't afford fresh water these days." He appraised Cannert. "Eighty dollars for a week?"

"Done," Cannert said. He took out a worn billfold and paid, letting the man see the thick sheaf of currency inside.

Cannert had hoped for a registration book so he could check for Martha's name but was handed a card instead. He filled it out and signed it "William T. Jones." The motel man inspected it and raised his eyebrows a fraction.

"Sure are a lot of Jones boys in this hard world," he said, not smiling.

Cannert nodded. "The 'T.' stands for Thurman. The kind of Jones you need to watch is the kind who comes with a woman and a bottle of liquor. I'm alone. I will be— all week. The only thing I drink is a bit of Canadian on special occasions." He looked around the Spartan office. "Where's closest and best to eat?"

"There's restaurants in town and there's a good one across from the pier right before you get to Citadel City." The motel man looked down at the card, and Cannert saw him then look out the office window to check the license number written on the card against the plate on the back of the Ford. Cannert smiled. Both were the same.

"Thanks," Cannert said shortly.

"Glad to have you with us, Mr. Jones," the motel man said appeasingly. He extended a heavy hand. "Name's Ed Bradford. The wife you saw when you arrived is Emma. Been here eleven years now. Trying to make do in lean times."

Cannert smiled and shook hands. "I understand about being cold. I'm out of Chicago. Retired a few months back. There was nothing and no one left to keep me in Illinois, so I'm wandering around, doing what I like." He nodded. "Golf some, fish some."

"You'll like the fishing hereabouts," Bradford said, "but there's no golf courses close." He went back to alertly watching the semideserted road out front, waiting patiently.

Cannert left the office. He unloaded his bags and golf clubs from the car, leaving only the fishing gear. He then drove to the edge of the small town a few miles away. It was now almost dark, too late to fish, but he found the restaurant near the pier and ate pleasantly enough there. Fishing talk came from nearby booths and he listened. He tipped the waitress the correct amount and played the role he knew best, remaining unnoticed.

When he departed, it was full, moonless dark outside. He drove back to the motel. There was only one new tourist car parked in front of a unit. Five rented, twenty-three vacant. A few children splashed in the dimly illuminated pool.

Cannert entered his room. He drew the shades and checked things over. Someone had gone through his bags. Only a watchful man would have noticed, but Cannert was careful. The roll of one-ounce gold Maple Leafs he'd left on one side of a bag was tilted wrong. Some of his clothes had been subtly moved around, then smoothed back.

Cannert turned out his lights and undressed. He smiled in the darkness. He felt Martha was very close to him here. Losing her had put purpose into what was left of life.

He hurt, so he took a strong pill.

He then slept deeply, without dreams.

The next morning he went again to the pier. He ate scrambled eggs and toast and then fished the day away. He was an indifferent fisherman, but a man had to fit into some mold. What he caught he gave away or threw back in when he was certain he wasn't observed.

He skipped lunch but ate an early dinner and drove back to the motel. Again, there were only a few tourist cars.

He went to his room and changed into his bathing suit and then walked slowly to the pool. A few children frolicked in the water, watched by their parents. The weather was muggy. Cannert put a cautious toe in the pool. The water was as warm as blood.

Ed Bradford came outside the office and watched him, smiling a little.

"How's the fishing?" he asked.

"Pretty fair," Cannert said. "I caught a few good ones, but I gave them away. Would you want any fish if I catch them tomorrow?"

Bradford nodded. "On one condition. This place will be dead tomorrow night. Sundays are. You bring the fish, and Em will cook for us. Maybe we could even have a drink of Canadian first?"

Cannert smiled. "That would be fine. You're very kind to a cold country stranger."

"A kindred spirit," Bradford said, still watching him. Cannert saw he'd noticed the long scar that ran down from upper belly to a hiding place deep in the swim trunks.

"That looks like a bad one."

"Car wreck," Cannert lied. "Slid on the ice. Lucky to be alive." It was, in truth, the place where they'd last opened him after the chemotherapy had failed and the radiation treatments had ended. They'd opened and then sewed him back, then given him the terminal news.

In the morning, Cannert left early. Only two tourist cars remained. Cannert drove for about a mile, found a turn-off spot, and parked his Ford behind a billboard. He walked back up the beach toward the motel.

From a vantage point behind a hummock of sand, he waited until the last tourist car had departed. Then he watched. In a while, Ed Bradford and his wife came out. They put a sign in the office window and then chugged off in a late-model Chevrolet.

Cannert patiently waited them out of sight and then walked to the motel. He checked the guest rooms and the office as he walked to his own room, but there was no one. He turned back. The sign on the office door read, "Gone to church. Closed all day today."

The office door was locked, but Cannert found a window which squeakily came up. He entered and searched quickly through the office. The safe was locked, but he had no real interest in it anyway. He wanted, most of all, to see the registration cards of those who'd come before him, but a quick search failed to turn them up.

He did find several things. In the kitchen, hidden behind the salt and flour, there was a small can of strychnine. Cannert opened it. About half was left. He emptied the can into a toilet and flushed it away. He filled the can back to the same level with salt. The salt didn't closely resemble the strychnine, but it was the closest thing he could find.

He put the can back and prowled some more. He found a .38 caliber revolver in a drawer. It was old and rusty but loaded with fresh-looking ammunition. Cannert left it loaded but knocked the firing pin off with a hammer he found in the kitchen. He took the firing pin with him when he left and dropped it in the sand near where he'd parked his car.

The exercise of walking and the excitement of breaking in had tired him so that he felt slightly faint. He took another strong pill and rested. He got out his vial of sleeping pills and broke up a dozen of them. He took the remainder and put them in his shirt pocket, then ground the broken bits into fine powder and put the powder back in the vial. All the time he was doing the grinding, he kept watch from his hiding place. When he saw Ed and Emma go past in their car, he waited until they vanished and then pulled his Ford out and went to the pier.

He wondered if he'd figured out what they had in store for him and hoped he had. If not, life was a gamble he was already losing.

Fishing was good at the pier. He caught three decent fish and put them on a stringer in his bucket.

Once, during the long afternoon when his stomach had quieted, he got a sandwich from the restaurant and then drove back to the pull-off place. He ate the sandwich and then walked the sands back to his hummock where he could check the motel. The Bradford car was parked behind the office, and there were no other cars. Out front, the neon no-vacancy sign glowed.

There was nothing else, but he knew they were in there waiting. Cannert smiled.

He returned to his car and drove once more to the fishing pier. Other fishermen around him talked about the weather and the fishing, but he mostly ignored them, waiting patiently for the afternoon to pass. When it was time to return to the motel, he filled the Ford with gas and also had an attendant fill the emergency five-gallon can he kept in the trunk.

Martha, maybe this time I've found you.

The church sign had been removed from the office door when he returned, but the no-vacancy sign still glowed. Cannert parked his car near the office and waved at Ed Bradford, who sat porcinely in khakis beside the pool.

Emma came out, smiling, and Cannert reflected that it was the first time he'd witnessed her with that expression. She took the fish he'd cleaned before he left the pier and vanished with them into the office.

Ed Bradford pointed at a bottle of good Canadian whiskey and a bucket of ice.

"Build yourself a drink," he said affably. "There's water for mix, or I can get you something from the Coke machine."

"Water's fine."

"Sit here, next to me. Tell me more about yourself. Tell me about how cold it was in Chicago." He smiled engagingly.

Cannert mixed a light drink and brought it to the pool. He sat in a chair near Bradford and rambled for a time. It was a story he'd told before. Some of it was true. There was no one for him now—no wife, no child, no brothers or sisters. He admitted to Bradford some of the truth about the long scar on his belly. He detailed the treatments and said he was now waiting out the time to see if they'd stopped the thing which grew inside. The last was a new lie. The answer was known.

They sipped their drinks companionably and watched the sun fall in the sky. Once, Emma came to the pool.

"Dinner in a few minutes," she said, smiling again at Cannert. "Do you drink coffee, Mr. Jones? Or tea?"

"Coffee—hot, black, and strong," Cannert said.

The answer widened her smile.

Ed Bradford kept adding to Cannert's drink, but Cannert was careful to sip it slowly.

When the sun was almost gone, they moved to the rooms behind the office. The kitchen table bore lighted candles. There was a festive bottle of wine.

"Let me open that for you," Cannert said jovially, seizing the opportunity. "Wine's better if it breathes a little."

He saw them smile knowingly at each other. He took the wine bottle and corkscrew to a dark counter and managed to dump his vial of powdered sleeping pills into the wine.

"I love wine but don't drink much of it these days," he said. "It seems to burn me." He held up his glass. "I would take another Canadian and water."

Ed Bradford fixed him a fresh one. It was dark brown with whiskey, and Cannert fought to control his stomach.

They ate companionably. The Bradfords copiously toasted their wine with his Canadian.

"No business at all tonight?" Cannert asked.

"Sometimes, on Sundays, I shut it off. All you get on Sundays are problems. Besides, it's a day of rest."

The meal was Cannert's fish. Emma had baked them in wine and doused them with lemon. They were good. On the side there was a crisp, green salad and tiny potatoes.

"New potatoes," Emma boasted. "And the salad's all fresh. No canned stuff. Me and Ed like to eat good."

Cannert nodded approval. "You people know how to live."

She brought him coffee—hot, black, and strong. Cannert sipped it and then idly added cream and sugar while they watched. The coffee was still salty, but he drank it.

"Tastes so strong it's almost bitter," he said appreciatively.

They nodded. Cannert could sense them waiting.

In a short while, he could see they were growing sleepy. It was time.

"I had a wife once," he said conversationally.

"A wife?" Ed asked.

"Yes. She came down to Florida to find a place for us when I first took sick. Maybe she might have stopped here? She'd have been traveling alone under the name of Martha Cannert. Big woman, grey hair."

"She might have stayed here. I don't remember her." Bradford stirred uneasily. He tried to rise and had problems. "What's wrong with me?" he asked.

The two watched each other, ignoring Cannert.

"I put something in the wine," Cannert explained.

Ed Bradford made it ponderously to his feet. He staggered to the drawer which held the gun. He dug it out and aimed it at Cannert. He clicked it twice.

"I knocked the firing pin off your gun."

The motel man reversed the gun and came toward him, but Cannert easily eluded him.

"It's only a sleeping powder," he told the two of them soothingly. "I need to know about my Martha. I think she stopped here. Maybe you killed her? That's what you had in mind for me, isn't it?"

"Still do," Ed Bradford muttered. "We'll wake up. You won't."

Cannert bent over, acting out inner pain. "Something hurts bad."

"It's the strychnine," Emma said triumphantly. "I put a lot in your coffee. You haven't got long."

"And Martha?" he pleaded.

"Maybe we got her, too. We do someone now and then. I think there was someone like that." She gave him a sleepy, apologetic look. "We have to do this to survive, you know. We can't fail again. We can't go back where it's cold. We've got to make it here, and times have gotten bad. So, now and then, we do someone, someone alone. Someone like you. We bury them at sea or under the sand. We sell the car or call the junk man for it. The Mister"—she nodded at her husband—"knows how."

"My Martha was a tall woman. She wore little half glasses and bright clothes. She drove a '76 Plymouth with Illinois plates." He thought for a moment. "It would have been about nine months ago."

Emma started to snore. Cannert moved from her to Ed and shook him. His eyes opened.

"Did you kill her?" he asked.

"We'll wake up," Bradford repeated. "You won't."

Cannert alternately searched the office and tried to shake one or the other of the Bradfords awake. The only results he achieved from the Bradfords were moans and mumbles and threshings about.

He found nothing in the office to convince him Martha had been a motel guest at Mom's. He did find guest cards in a file in the back of a drawer under the desk. He went through them. The cards had gaps in their consecutive numbers, and he theorized they'd destroyed the cards of those they'd killed. Going back a year, he counted eight missing numbers including his own. He scattered the remaining cards about the rooms.

He waited until the moon was down outside, waited until he'd not heard a passing car along the road that fronted the motel for a long time. Then he loaded his car and drove it to the darkened front of the office, after washing and toweling every place he might have touched in his own room.

He went back inside the office area. Ed Bradford now snored loudly, but Emma lay unmoving, her breathing shallow. He tried to awaken them, but without success.

Cannert doused the office and the rooms back of it with

the contents of the emergency can of gas he'd purchased earlier.

From outside the front door he tossed a match. He dodged away from the sudden surge of flame and heat.

He drove to the highway. Behind him, from there, he could see flames already breaking out from under the eaves on the pool side of the office area.

He drove north and pulled off the road again about a mile away at a higher place. By the time he heard distant fire engines, the flames were crackling against the sky.

He started his car again and drove sedately on.

Someplace, down another road, there'd be another motel, another place Martha might have stayed. He decided to drive east. He thought about new methods for the next place. This time there'd be no angry rifle shots because someone had looked through his bag, then done nothing else. This time there'd be no arson. An idea about dynamite came and made him smile. He knew about dynamite.

A man in his condition needed to stay occupied.

Trial

Senator Adams called me into his office early that morning. He nodded me into an ancient overstuffed chair, parted a place in his lawbooks so that he could peer through at me, and then began. I could sense he wasn't very happy.

"I want you to help me defend Russell Quinn next week, Robak. I'll pick the jury and be with you most of the trial, but I have some problems which may not let me do all the trial with you."

I looked moodily out his sooty window at Bington's fall. Rough winds were blowing varicolored leaves off the courthouse-lawn trees and covering the ground below. The wino crowd, which met daily on the courthouse wall to split a bottle or three of muscatel, weather permitting, seemed unfazed. I wasn't.

"That's *your* murder case," I said uncertainly.

"I see you remember that much about it. It's a start," the senator said sarcastically. A state senator, once elected, later defeated, in my area is "Senator" forever. "Here's the file," he said, handing it to me.

I took it from him. It was bulky. "What's the problem?" I asked, still doubtful.

He looked down at his desk. "I had some chest pains last night and went to the hospital emergency room." He held up a hand. "Nothing real bad, but my doctor ordered me to take it easier. I told him about the trial. The prosecutor and I both want it tried. First the doctor told me to continue it, but Russell has been in jail for seven months. I explained that. So then he ordered me not to try it and have you do it all. I worked out the compromise I'm now spelling out for you."

"All right," I said. I took the file, not happy about it but willing now that all had been revealed. I knew that the senator's health was, at best, questionable. I still didn't much like getting involved late in a murder case and I was still at the stage of my life where I believed people were automatically guilty just because the state had arrested and charged them.

Russell Quinn was *the* local gambler and I knew him a little. He was a big, bulky man with black hair and strong arms. His reputation for peace and sobriety was spotty, but his reputation for tough honesty was first-class. Seven months before he'd been arrested for knifing another local gambler, Odds Jacobson, after an all-night poker game above Jacobson's pool hall. There were no witnesses to the offense itself, but there were other players available from the fatal game who'd heard threats made by Russell to Odds. Odds had won, Russell had lost. Russell had thereupon threatened to kill Odds, accusing him of cheating. Russell's knife was found later by the body. There was no money on the body, but Russell, apprehended at his home, had a wad of cash. Circumstantial, but probably enough.

The senator had made some notes in the file. One of them read, "No Other Enemies?" Another said, "Five Players?" A third was dim and I had to lean down to read it. "Set Up?" it asked.

I went back to his office to ask him about the notes, but he was gone. Virginia, our harassed secretary, said he'd gone home for the day.

I walked back to my own office and reopened the file. There was a list of witnesses for the state. Leaving out the

police who'd investigated and the doctors who'd examined Odds's body, there were only three witnesses who
seemed worth investigating: the other three cardplayers.

Senator Adams had already done that. There were depositions inside the file. I read them. They seemed mild
enough. They described the card game, the stakes, that
Odds had won, and that Russell had lost his money and
then his temper. Each cardplayer had stated where he'd
gone at the conclusion of the game. The senator had put
question marks by two of the names, excepting out only a
Sam Shannon. I read the depositions again and thought I
might have some idea of the senator's thinking. There
were three other suspects, good suspects. All that tied our
man Quinn to the case were their statements and the
knife.

On the front of the file Senator Adams had printed, "See
Coger Rock." Rock was the prosecuting attorney, and a
good and fair one.

We began trial on a blustery Tuesday morning. Outside
a driving rain scoured Bington's streets. Inside Coger Rock
quickly proved that Odds was dead, that the knife found
beside him was Russell's property, with his initials on it,
and that there'd been bad blood between Odds and Russell. Pictures of a bloody Odds, on a slab, were shown to
the jurors. The senator sat beside me, his old prune face
calm and seemingly not much interested. On the far side
of the counsel table Russell Quinn sat, his face impassive.
Now and then he'd make a note on a yellow pad and hand
it to the senator. Behind Russell two deputy sheriffs sat
watching.

The senator first came a little alive when the state pre-
sented a fingerprint expert. He leaned forward and listened to him testify.

"I found a fingerprint on the small blade of the knife,"

the expert said. "I checked it and it was Russell Quinn's print." Prosecutor Rock, huge in his best black suit, wheezingly set up a projector and showed the print on the knife blade, then showed the jury another taken from Russell Quinn and had the expert testify learnedly about their sameness. I saw jurors nodding.

Senator Adams leaned to me. "Ask this cookie which blade of the knife killed Odds Jacobson."

I did, politely enough, when Prosecutor Rock was done with his impressive show and tell.

"I don't know," he said haughtily. "All I did was what I was supposed to do—check fingerprints. Those of Russell Quinn were the only ones I found on the knife I examined."

"And that print on the small blade was the only print you found?"

"Yes. There were smudges other places, but no prints."

Dr. Katen, who'd done the autopsy, had the information the senator wanted.

"He was killed with the long blade of the knife. Someone stabbed him five times in and around the heart. The stab wounds were deep, too deep for the short blade, but they fit with the long blade of the knife. Once the blade was withdrawn wounds of that nature contract. Odds's fatal wounds had done that but could not have been the work of the short blade." He nodded. "The wounds would have had to have been made by a strong person."

The jury examined Russell Quinn and saw what they needed as far as strength was concerned.

"How strong?" I asked.

The doctor shrugged. "What I mean by that is that the wounds couldn't have been inflicted by an eighty-year-old woman."

Senator Adams nodded at me, satisfied. "Now we wait until they call the other poker players," he whispered. He reached in his briefcase. "They're strong, too. Here are their arrest records, Robak. Take them home and read them over tonight." He nodded mysteriously. "The prosecutor and I have already been over them."

"Yes, sir," I said.

"You seem happier than you once were about this case," he said, smiling, but only a little.

"I think you have something up your sleeve," I said.

He looked at me and I couldn't read anything in his old lizard eyes. "Read the arrest records. And tomorrow we must warn Judge Steinmetz and the prosecutor that there's a separation of witnesses in effect and that we don't want the witnesses talking among themselves. Perhaps the judge might even put a deputy in the hall to make certain that doesn't happen."

"Why bother?" I asked.

He smiled but would say no more.

I went home to my apartment and read and then reread the records of the three other witnesses. Reading them was about like going to a seminar on all the various offenses of man. The three had been involved in a variety of crimes.

I kept waking up in the night and going over the cross-examination I planned. Between them the three witnesses had been convicted of everything from manslaughter to pickpocketing. None of the three was clean.

I planned and then slept. I awoke early, when the sun first streaked the sky with light, and went over what I'd read again. Outside the day had awakened cold and there was a hint of snow in the air. I walked to the courthouse.

The first of the three was Sam Shannon. Coger Rock led him through testimony about the game, about Quinn's pique at losing, and about the threats which had been made.

"He said he'd kill Odds. He said Odds had cheated."
Shannon nodded righteously. "I didn't see no cheating."

Rock stopped and left him to us. Senator Adams nodded
me on and I went after Sam Shannon.

"Did you ever threaten Odds Jacobson, Mr. Shannon?"

"Not me. I try to get along with everyone."

"Did you get along with one Edward Black on or about
the eighth day of April five years ago?"

"Objection," Coger said for the record. We'd already
argued out what was available to us in evidence in a hearing out of the presence of the jury earlier. And Rock and
the senator had both seemed very friendly about their
arguments, which was a bit unusual.

"You may answer," Judge Steinmetz said, looking down.

"Me and Eddo had some problems. I did my time for
that."

"Didn't you attack Edward Black with a knife on that
date and kill him?"

"Sure, but it was a fair fight."

"Did Odds Jacobson fight fair when you took Quinn's
knife to him the night you killed him?" I asked.

"I never did it to him. Me and Odds was friends. Ask
anyone."

"Did you leave Odds's premises with the other two players in the game besides Odds and Quinn Russell?"

"No. They went their way, I went mine. We're not that
close."

I couldn't get him to change anything. I tried various
devices, trying to trap him, but nothing worked. Finally I
caught the senator's nod and went to the counsel table.

"Enough," he whispered. "This one has a good alibi for
the rest of that evening. Three people came by and picked
him up at the pool hall when the game was over and were
with him the rest of the night. Ask for a short recess."

I looked up at Steinmetz. "Could we have five minutes to confer before the next witness is called, Your Honor?"

"All right," Judge Steinmetz said, looking at us curiously.

When the jury had gone out Senator Adams asked, "Do you think you can figure a way to make the next witness very angry at you, Robak?"

"I can try." I looked around the old courtroom, thinking about it. Making people mad was one of my gifts.

"Keep working on him until you do. Be your normal self, nasty, sarcastic, disagreeable. Accuse him, confront him, and make him angry at you. I'm told he has a hair-trigger temper."

"Yes, sir," I said, wondering why.

"I want to talk to Coger Rock for a moment now," he said.

I watched him walk over to the other counsel table and confer with Rock, who listened and nodded. The whole thing was confusing to me.

The next witness for the State was Charles "Chuck" Whiteway and what I'd read on him wasn't very encouraging. At one time he'd been a very good daylight burglar in the area in and around Bington. He'd also been a strong-arm bandit. He'd gone to prison twice and had spent time in most of the area jails, usually for fighting. Lately he'd seemed to semiretire, had taken a job as a combination bartender-bouncer in one of Bington's tough bars. He was large and fortyish and moved with great energy and vigor. His eyes seemed to view the world around him with contempt.

Once again Prosecutor Coger Rock led him through the story concerning the poker game and dug it out of him. He seemed reluctant to testify and I thought I'd use that against him.

I got him after an hour of wheedling by Coger.

"You seem reluctant to testify, Mr. Whiteway," I said. "Why is that?"

He nodded at me. "Both Quinn and Odds were friends of mine."

"I'll bet. How did you get to know Odds? In prison?"

"Odds was never in prison, bud."

"I see. Did you get to know him by burglarizing his place? Or maybe beating him up? Or robbing him?"

He shook his head, his face reddening a little.

"And you say Russell Quinn here is or was a friend of yours, too?" I asked.

"That's right."

"Having you for a friend isn't of much help to either one of them. One's dead, the other's here on trial for murder with you testifying against him."

"I was subpoenaed."

"Anybody pay you to be here?"

He pulled at his collar and glared at me. "Of course not."

"You're too honest for that, aren't you?" I asked, grinning superciliously at him.

"I'm honest enough," he said doggedly.

"I don't think there's any truth in you, Mr. Whiteway. I think you stole for so long that it's your way of life. And I think now you're trying to steal—"

It was enough. He came up out of the witness chair and aimed one my way. I ducked inside it and then the bailiff and one of the deputies had him. Steinmetz pounded his gavel.

"Take that man to jail and let him cool off. You can call him back later if you want, Mr. Robak."

I nodded.

At our counsel table Senator Adams looked pleased. I tried to read Coger Rock's expression but couldn't.

We insisted on moving ahead and so Coger called his last witness, Don Bradberry. He was the youngest of the players and he came through as a very unctuous witness. His record indicated he'd been a sneak thief since his youth, a pickpocket, and a con man. He had earnest blue eyes that he partially hid behind large hornrims. I guessed him to be thirty, tall, built like a football end. Coger finished with him in half an hour.

The senator whispered, "I'll take this one."

I nodded, surprised. He seemed alive again. When the prosecution finished he was on his feet circling Bradberry like some old, still savage bird of prey.

"We've had some startling things happen here today, Mr. Bradberry. The last witness was taken to jail."

Bradberry nodded warily.

"Can you think of any reason for that?"

"No, sir," he said nervously and waited.

"Think hard," the senator said, grinning coldly at him.

Bradberry shrugged.

"Could it be because he told us you stole Russell Quinn's knife, which meant he'd lied in his deposition? Could that be it?"

"If he told you that, he lied," Bradberry said, looking at the senator with hate in his eyes.

"He told us a lot of things," the senator said.

Coger Rock started to get up and then sat back down. He shook his head like a bewildered boxer and glanced down at his counsel table.

Bradberry looked at the senator. "I picked the knife for him. He gave me a hundred for it. He said if I ever told he'd kill me." He shook his head in disgust at the perfidy of men. "And then he breaks and tells. That's all I know."

The senator turned to me and then to the prosecutor. "Enough?" he asked Coger.

The prosecutor nodded.

Later I sat with both of them in the downtown Moose. "You set me up," I said to both of them.

"Coger wasn't satisfied and neither was I," the senator said. "He agreed to give me a little leeway. He did and here we are." He smiled his sour lemon smile. "No one likes to convict an innocent man. The evidence that Coger had against Russell Quinn was enough to convict with, but not enough to completely convince Coger."

Rock nodded. He drank his diet cola, perspiring freely despite the air conditioning. He smiled at me. "I may never do that sort of thing again. The best man of that bunch of poker players was Russell Quinn. He's mean and a brawler. I thought he might have beaten Odds to death, but not have knifed him. The senator thought, after the depositions, that it was Whiteway. But no one was going to change things without someone tinkering with the process. So I let you guys have a little leeway." He looked at the senator and then at his watch. "It's time," he said.

"Where are you off to?" I asked.

"A poker game at Judge Steinmetz's house. I can promise that none of today's players will be there. Care to join us?"

Truly Yours, John R. Jacks

There was a full November moon up there in the night sky and Jacks, who kept up on things like that, knew it, but the moon was dimmed by thin, late-fall clouds. He pressed a button on the luxury car's dash and a computer readout told him it was thirty degrees outside. *Cold.*

He liked the big car and the feeling of power it gave him. It seemed almost an extension of himself. He pushed the accelerator down a little and tasted the added speed.

The road ahead appeared deserted, but then Jacks saw the hitchhiker. He'd read in area newspapers that it wasn't safe or smart to pick them up, especially on semideserted roads, but he'd done it before. And it was an unusually cold night for anyone to be out. He slowed.

The man who opened the passenger door of the Cadillac was thin and gray, older in appearance than Jacks. He was dressed in worn jeans and wore a thick but threadbare coat. He smiled ingratiatingly.

"Thanks," he said, climbing in. He smelled vaguely of mothballs and burning leaves. "For a while I didn't think anyone would ever pick me up. Not much traffic on this road, what with all the interstates nearby. Nice of a young man like you to pick up an old man like me."

"I'm going as far as Bargersville," Jacks said, smiling back. He nodded at the backseat of his car. "I sell supplies to hospitals, emergency rooms, and doctors all over five states and I wanted to get to Bargersville tonight so I could make an early start in the morning. You can make better time on the back roads this time of year. And they're far more interesting to drive."

"Drug salesman?" the man asked.

"No. Equipment. Small stuff, retractors, clamps scalpel blades." He smiled. "If I was into selling drugs I'd never pick anyone up." He extended his right hand. "Name's Jacks, John R. Jacks."

The other man nodded and shook hands, his own hand cold in Jacks's warm palm. "I'm Joe Bell. Your accent sounds British."

"So it is a bit," Jacks said, surprised at the man's acuteness. "I was born and raised in the east part of the finest city in the world, London, but I've been all over. One never loses one's birth heritage, I suppose."

"I've lived a lot of places, too," Bell said. "Some of them not very nice. Hospitals. Rest homes. That sort of thing." His voice was bitter.

Jacks nodded politely while Bell settled deeper into the passenger seat of the Cadillac.

Jacks got the car rolling well again, seeing the speedometer pass fifty miles an hour. "Beastly night to be hitchhiking."

Bell smiled sleepily and nodded. "I guess I'm a bit more than your average hitchhiker." He put his right hand casually in his coat pocket and brought out a small revolver. "I do people for a hobby—men, women, kids, it makes me no difference." He looked out at the road ahead. "About a mile or so up there's a side road that I know. You pull in there. Then you and I will have a bit of fun before I leave you behind and take your car. Maybe with it I can get away from here, away from where they're undoubtedly already looking for me, although I've only been gone for a day or so."

"They're looking for you?" Jacks asked.

Bell nodded. "Yes. You're a real saviour."

"What sort of fun are you after?" Jacks asked.

"You'll do things for me and I'll do things to you," Bell said. "Great fun. I'll like it. You may not. One never knows about pretty young men like you." His lip curled.

Jacks nodded, understanding. The spring knife he kept up his right sleeve, ready to flick down at the right movement, felt warm and good against his skin. The juices inside him quickened. Perhaps there'd be a chance.

"I take it you've engaged in this sort of antisocial conduct before?" he asked in a low voice, scandalized by the thought of it.

"Many times," Bell said. He shrugged, his attitude almost apologetic. "They lock me up when they catch me, but I'm difficult to catch and hard to hold. They say I'm insane, but I know I'm not. One doctor said what I did was an irresistible impulse. I liked the phrase when I heard it. I'm afraid my impulse is something I just have to do now and then. It was very kind of you to stop for me. Now I'm going to repay you."

"I don't want repayment," Jacks said. "You can take the car and what's in it. Just let me go, let me out. I won't say anything to anyone."

"But I must repay you," Bell answered mockingly.

They drove on. In the other lane a car approached, the first one Jacks had seen in the better part of an hour. There were lights mounted on the top of the approaching vehicle.

"Careful now," Bell said. "That's a state police car. Do anything wrong and I'll shoot you now and spoil all our fun-to-be."

Jacks shook his head. "I'm not even tempted." He drove steadily onward. He nodded curiously at Bell. "But think about it yourself. What would or could you do if I drove my auto into the other lane? If you shot me you'd probably die also in the crash. Or the police would have caught you."

"Don't be silly. You'd die too."

"Realistic is the way I view it," Jacks pointed out. "I doubt you intend me to live through this anyway."

They drove on in silence. Bell watched Jacks carefully, perhaps not as sure of him as he'd been at first. Jacks smiled at him to lull him back to a sense of security.

"You don't seem afraid," Bell said. "You should be praying."

"I gave up praying years ago," Jacks said. "I'm a fatalist. What will be will be. Shouldn't your mile be about up?"

"There's the side road now," Bell said pointing, then looking quickly back at Jacks, watching him carefully.

"Yes," Jacks said. "I see it." He pulled into a narrow lane and drove bumpily back about fifty feet from the highway.

"Far enough," Bell said, excited again now. "Park the car right here. Get out on your side. Don't try to run. I'm very good with this gun."

"I'm sure you would be," said Jacks. He turned off his lights and opened his door carefully. He got out of the car. Even with the full moon behind thin clouds there was enough light to see. It was very cold, but the wind was still. Jacks smelled the coming of winter. Someplace close by an owl called its greeting to the two interlopers into its frigid world.

Jacks triggered the closed spring knife down into his hand. There was a button on top of it which let the blade slide down from inside the handle. He'd seen it in a small shop in Germany, liked it, and bought it. Years ago.

"Come around here to me," Bell said whiningly, quite excited now. "Come see the last of your life. Come to me."

Jacks complied docilely.

"Come close," Bell ordered. "So pretty," he crooned.

Jacks moved closer. He saw that the gun had vanished back into a pocket and that Bell now menacingly held a short pocket knife.

"I'm going to penetrate you a little and then there'll be your clothes to be removed," Bell whispered. He moved lovingly forward. "Be good," he pleaded. He raised the knife hesitantly. "Some of them just die. Don't do that. Fun first."

Jacks waited motionless until Bell was very close. Then he pressed the handle button and heard the tiny snicking sound. He brought the long knife up swiftly so that it pressured the hollow under Bell's jaw. He countered Bell's thrust with his free hand, locking Bell's arm. Bell looked at him with shocked eyes. Jacks let the point of his long knife dig in a quarter of an inch, drawing blood.

"Make me uneasy in any way and I'll let this blade glide up through your tongue and into your brain," Jacks said. "You can already feel that it's very sharp, not like the dirty thing you carry." He smiled at Bell. "You drop your little toy and then take off your coat. That will put your revolver beyond your immediate reach should you be tempted to try to use it."

Bell followed the instructions. He stood shivering in the cold, a thin old man out on a night much too cold for him, still excited, but now in a different way.

"If you're going to turn me in there's a police station in Bargersville. In a few weeks I'd probably have turned myself in anyway. It's getting too cold to stay out long. Next time I'll try to remember to escape in the summer. They watch me close for a while and then they forget." He smiled. "And away I go."

Jacks nodded, not very much interested.

"You turn me in and they'll take me back to the asylum," Bell said conversationally. He smiled. "It's not so bad there and maybe I'll get out again. I have my scrapbook at the asylum for the lonely, cold nights. I keep it hidden so that only I get to see it. Lots of lovely news clips. Some about me, some about others like me." He nodded, agitated a little. "It's very cold without my coat. Can't we get back in the car now?"

"Maybe in a few moments," Jacks said. "I'd wager you would get out again, but I'm not going to turn you in. I haven't got the time or the inclination to come back for hearings and perhaps a trial." Jacks shook his head. "Gentlemen like you are a hazard." He pointed out at the Cadillac. "My vehicle is parked so close to the road that if that state chap who was going the other way came back and drove past he'd likely see it and us."

"I've used this place before and not been caught," Bell said. "Back in the bushes there's a body from yesterday. Would you like to see it? Very nice body. An old, talkative lady."

"No," Jacks said.

"You'd have joined her. Then one more. I like to do them in threes. Lucky, you know."

Jacks shook his head in wonder. "And you never bothered to examine me for a weapon. You took me for granted. I'm surprised you've lived as long as you have."

"Most people do what I say," Bell said. "They're too scared and shocked not to do it. They think maybe I'll let them go if they do exactly what I tell them." He moved his head cautiously, not liking the knife at his throat. "That hurts me. Where'd the knife come from? You made it appear like something out of a magic trick."

"From back the years," Jacks said. He shook his head. "Random killers like you, sexual deviates, thrill murderers, psychopaths, give the civilized world a bad odor." He pulled the sharp knife slightly away.

Bell seemed to relax a little as he was able to lower his head. He rubbed the cut spot on his neck, seemingly puzzled by it. He put a bloody fingertip from the wound in his mouth. "It never seems to hurt when they cut each other on TV. Or I never thought it hurt until I killed my first one." He shook his head wonderingly. "She screamed a lot."

Jacks heard a sound approaching from far away. He shoved the knife close to Bell's throat again.

Both of the men stood unmoving while out on the road a truck went past, traveling fast, unseeing, not slowing.

When it was still again, Jacks said calmly and reasonably, "One must learn how, when, and why to kill, how to follow the stars from old books that were banned and burned whenever they were found. I read the last survivor of those old dark god books before it was also destroyed. That was a long time ago. That book taught me how a man could stay young forever. I've followed what it taught. I've lived in a dozen countries. I like this one best. Very easy here, very relaxed. Lots of serial killers to keep the police busy. Lots of violence. I'm going to stay and prosper forever. In a moment I'm going to get my own little kit of sharp, delicate things from among those items in my backseat I sell to doctors and hospitals and emergency rooms."

Bell shook his head. "You can't kill me. Only I can kill." His eyes were positive. "I am the power. No one else can kill, Mr. John R. Jacks, whoever you are."

"I can," Jacks said surely. "You see, I need certain portions of you for my required periodic rituals." He smiled. "I first learned the trade as a young man in London in 1888. Then it was women only, but my sorcery now allows men." He bowed slightly. "I am in your debt. You will be the latest to help me remain forever young."

Bell shrieked once as the sharp knife entered and penetrated.

Jacks said mockingly, the doggerel coming to him instantaneously, as it always had since those early great times in London when he'd written to the newspapers of the times:

"You forgot both Jacks in my name, Mr. Bell,
But those Jacks should have been a sure tipper.
So remember well, as you head for hell,
That the R. in my name stood for 'Ripper.' "

All That Mattered

After eight years of married life, they'd adjusted to each
other's needs in many ways. Flora mostly needed to be
treasured, Zirbeck mostly needed to know that she and
Joey were there for him.

One example was the phone calls which came in the
middle of the night.

They came at various times, at midnight, at 2 A.M., at
five. They came several times a month at least and sometimes, in the heat of the summer, when tempers were up
and the city's windows open, as often as twice or three
times in a single week.

Before their marriage, Zirbeck had indulged in the luxury of allowing the phone to go through five or six rings
before forcing himself back to consciousness and rolling
toward it and bitching only half jokingly at the guy from
the precinct at the other end of the line.

And early in their time together, in the year before Joey
was born, Flora would snap awake almost as soon as the
ringing began. She would lie there stiffly while her husband dealt with the call, praying that this would be one of
the times when he could hang up and nestle close and hold
her and she could drift back to sleep in his arms. Those
times were the exceptions, though. Almost always the late-
night calls meant his presence was required at a crime
scene, and she would not see him again until morning, if
then. *If ever.*

"Gotta go," he'd tell her, and she would embrace him

tightly for the few moments he could spare her, knowing that this embrace, these moments, could turn out to be the final ones she would ever have with him. The fear was irrational. She told herself that time and time again, but the self-counseling never did any good. Sometimes when he was gone she'd lie awake telling herself not to worry, not to worry, and then worry until dawn smeared the sky outside their bedroom window and it was time to get up and get dressed. Other times she was able to get back to sleep again after he left. Those times were the worst.

Those were the times she had the nightmare.

They had adjusted, though, over the years, and now Zirbeck would snatch up the receiver in the middle of the first ring and keep his end of the conversation terse and whispered. Flora would sleep on—peacefully it seemed—as his lips brushed her forehead with a kiss and he slipped out of bed and into his clothes and away.

But she still had the nightmare. The soft click of the bedroom door closing behind him registered somewhere deep within her as she slept, and it was at that moment that the nightmare began.

It was always the same bad dream. A dark alley, her husband at one end and a man with a gun at the other, a shot ringing out and a body sprawling lifelessly on the slick asphalt. Then the scene abruptly shifted and she was home. Two uniformed men she didn't know stood at the door with their hats in their hands. One of them wore a heavy gold ring, she'd always notice, a golden dragon with its tail twisted around his finger, and it was that one who'd tell her that her husband wasn't coming home, was not coming home, was never coming home.

Even now, after eight years of married life, dawn found her awake and trembling each time her husband went off in the night.

It was 1:17 A.M. The telephone rang, and Zirbeck came awake and scooped it up almost before the sound began. He checked to see if Flora was still sleeping. She was, she always was, and he said his name softly into the mouthpiece.

"I told you to call 'em off," a harsh voice rasped in his ear. "I warned you, Zirbeck, but you didn't listen."

Zirbeck cursed silently. He recognized the voice from countless fruitless interrogations over the years. Lost Tony Luvisi, a nasty small-timer with little imagination but a sadistic streak a continent wide. They'd never been able to hang anything big on Lost Tony so that it stuck, not so far, but they were drawing closer. There'd been a series of armed robberies lately. All the places robbed were jewelry stores. Several of the owners and employees had been cruelly and unnecessarily roughed up by a lone bandit in a ski mask. The heists had Lost Tony's name written all over them, and police officers throughout the city were putting in overtime digging for evidence enough against him to hold up in court. Zirbeck was especially concerned as most of the stickups had taken place in his precinct. Tony *had* warned him a week ago, with an anonymous letter which had wound up in the closest circular file.

Now this. Lost Tony obviously didn't know the police as well as they knew him. Zirbeck laid the receiver down gently and sat on the edge of the bed for a time with his hand on it, in case Tony should decide to try the number again.

But the phone remained silent. Minutes ticked by. Zirbeck let himself lie back and eased his arm around his wife and held her against him gently. Tomorrow, he'd have to do something about Lost Tony's threats.

Tomorrow.

That night was one of the good ones, when Flora didn't dream her nightmare.

He came into the kitchen knotting his tie as Flora was pouring coffee. She smiled at him and said nothing about the phone call in the middle of the night. In her pink robe with its billowing sleeves she looked like a teenager, and when she turned back to the range he crept up behind her and wrapped her in a bear hug that made her squeal.

Joey, eating cereal, giggled. He liked mornings a lot better when Daddy was home. The other days, when he was at work, Mamma seemed so sad and anxious. He was always sorry and he'd ask her what was wrong, but most times she'd stare at him for a while and make her lips tight and shake her head and say "Nothing" like she was about to cry or something, like Mary, the little girl next door, whose mother was so thin and sick. Mary said her mother had "big sea," but she didn't really know what that meant, though she acted as if she did. Mary was kind of a showoff.

Zirbeck planted a kiss on his son's cheek and took a seat at the table. "Who gets to go to kindergarten this morning?" he asked the room at large.

"Me!" Joey said proudly. Kindergarten was an adventure. He liked kindergarten.

"And me," Flora added. "I'm going to drop him off."

"The buses not running?"

She shook her head. "I'm going that way anyway, so I thought I'd drop him off. I want to take my car down to Foster's Garage and have them check the brakes."

"Brakes," Joey confirmed.

Zirbeck sipped coffee. "What's the matter with the brakes?"

She shrugged. "I guess they need adjustment." She brought two plates of eggs and toast to the table and sat. "I have to put my foot almost to the floor to come to a full stop."

"You could need new brake pads, honey. I'll take it in

with me this morning and let the boys in the garage look it over."

"Sweetheart," Flora said, frowning, "that's not what the police garage is there for. I'll drop Joey off and take the car to Foster's. It's no trouble for me and no one looking sideways at you."

Zirbeck crammed more toast in his mouth. He chewed and then swallowed. He grinned at Joey. "See that? Don't talk with your mouth full at kindergarten, right? It's bad manners." He turned back to his wife. "You say that, but the fellas are happy to do it. Not for me. If it was my car they'd file a union grievance if I asked them to put air in the tires, but they *like* getting the chance to pay you back a little for the good baked stuff you send in. Lemme take your car in with me this morning and Joey take the bus."

Now Joey was frowning. "I want Mamma to take me," he said, wondering if he was going to lose this one.

Mamma came to his rescue. "I'll take you, Joey. In Daddy's car instead of mine." She nodded at Zirbeck. "You can keep the boys at the garage happy. I've got some shopping to do, so it's just as well I take a dependable car."

He was at Davidson's Jewelers, scene of the latest robbery, when the call came in to the precinct. It was more than half an hour later before a patrol car pulled up and double-parked in front of the glass display window.

A heavyset detective in a poorly cut brown suit stepped out of the passenger side of the black-and-white. He looked through the plate-glass door toward the back of the shop, to where Zirbeck was listening to Perelli question a little guy who was obviously Davidson. Zirbeck was really engrossed in the dialogue. The detective knew how badly he wanted Lost Tony Luvisi out of circulation. And now this. My God, now this.

The detective sighed and pushed the door open. They

called him "Bad News Charley" because he did a lot of jobs like this.

A bell hanging from the transom rang and Davidson cut himself off in midsentence.

"Charley," said Zirbeck, examining him clinically. "What are *you* doing here?"

Charley cleared his throat. "Um, can I speak to you outside for a second, Lieutenant?"

Zirbeck tilted his head. "Sure, Charley. Go ahead without me, Perelli. Excuse me, Mr. Davidson." He walked up beside the older detective and lowered his voice. "What's wrong, Charley?"

"Come outside for a minute," Charley insisted and led him back out the door.

Then, standing there in the street at nine o'clock on a chilly April morning, Charley told Zirbeck about the car bomb.

He fixed himself a cup of tea for dinner. There was food in the house, fresh cooked food police wives had brought, but he didn't want to look at it. And in the freezer there'd be packages of three lamb chops, three ground-beef patties, three chicken breasts. In the refrigerator were Flora's low-cal sodas and special salad dressing, stuff she'd started buying when she'd put on those five extra pounds. Joey's favorite cookies and peanut butter and jelly were in the cabinets. Nothing was safe, but the cannister of tea bags on the Formica counter next to the stove seemed safest. He was the only one who ever drank tea.

He wasn't hungry or thirsty even for that, but he brewed himself a cup of tea anyway. To do something.

Flora and Joey. All that mattered in life. Gone. The house was quiet, very quiet.

The breakfast dishes were still on the table. Joey's cereal

was only half eaten. *The kid never does finish a meal,* he thought, *there's always something left over.*

Never does, there is. He corrected the grammar in his mind. *Never did. There was.*

He sat down in Joey's chair and tried a spoonful of cereal. It was terrible, all sugar and the milk soured. He dumped the rest of it in the trash and took his tea out to the living room.

It wasn't any better out there. They'd picked out the furniture together, piece by piece over the eight years of their marriage, chosen the wallpaper and painted the ceiling and hung the pictures. She was everywhere he looked in the room, every place he touched in the house, she and Joey. He could see and touch where they'd been, but he couldn't touch *them,* not anymore.

After a while he found himself leaning into his closet and staring at his clothes. His suits, shirts, trousers, and ties, the things he wore when he was at work, away from them and the house. He had no idea how long he'd been standing there staring. He saw his leather shoulder holster hanging on its peg with the .38-caliber revolver inside it. Then he was sitting on their bed, his bed, with the gun in his hands. He cradled it tenderly, as if it were a living thing.

The gun was loaded with five bullets, with an empty chamber under the hammer. He'd used it often enough in the line of duty but was proud of the fact that he'd never had to kill with it. He wondered if he could kill with it now. Fired into a mouth at the right angle a bullet would range upward and leave a huge hole in the skull where it exited. How would that compare with what had been done to Flora and Joey?

The expert at headquarters had told him six to eight sticks of dynamite had been wired to the ignition of his Valiant. They wouldn't let him see what the explosion had done to his wife and son, but he'd seen what it had done to the garage. That was enough.

They'd assured him downtown that Homicide was working on it, working hard. He'd given them what he had, but the list of people who might have hated him enough to put a bomb in his car was long. The call from Lost Tony told him everything he needed to know, but it wasn't evidence, wasn't proof.

When his vision cleared he was holding the gun with his finger inside the trigger guard. He wondered briefly what the bullet would taste like entering.

Then he said the word "no" aloud to the empty room. *I can't do it,* he thought, *I won't do it. I won't pull the trigger even though it's the thing I ought to do. Not me, not me.*

He got up from the bed and put the gun back in its holster.

"I want Lost Tony Luvisi," he told the squad next morning after roll call. "I don't want him persecuted or harassed and I don't want his civil rights violated, but I want him. Right and legal, just like I've always wanted him. Nothing has changed. We're going to try an unobtrusive twenty-four-hour stakeout on him, three men in unmarked cars working eight-hour shifts. Don't crowd him, just keep him in sight. Stay way back and don't make trouble. Homicide downtown will be checking him out and questioning him, but we've questioned Tony before and a lot of good that ever does. Sooner or later he'll try another jewelry store and maybe we'll get lucky. Don't screw it up: go completely by the book and treat him very gently. I want to be in the courtroom when a judge sends him away, I want to wave goodbye when he goes. I need three volunteers."

Every hand in the room went up.

Zirbeck nodded at the grim, loyal faces, at the raised arms. For the first time since he'd gotten the news he remembered he was alive. "Okay. Stevick," he said, "Perelli and Walsh. You take him the first week and we'll see how it goes." That was all he had to say, but somehow the word "dismissed" didn't seem to want him to speak it. "Thank you all," he said in its place.

The men filed quietly out of the room. Bad News Charley Walsh lagged behind. "Maybe you ought to stay home for a couple of days, Lieutenant? Just till— Ah, hell . . ."

"There's nothing for me there, Charley. I'm better off here."

Walsh pulled in a deep breath. "Thanks for picking me. I wanted you to pick me. Jesus, Al, it killed me yesterday to tell you."

"I know," Zirbeck said. He gripped the detective's shoulder and squeezed it gently.

Walsh turned to go. He was old and tired and ready for retirement, but when he turned back again for a moment, Zirbeck saw that his eyes were still questing and young.

"We'll get him, Al. We'll do it straight, just like you want, but we'll get him. Not for Flora and Joey; it's too late for them. But Luvisi is a menace, he's bad poison. We'll take him down for that. And for you, Al. We'll go after him for you."

Tony Luvisi shot pool in a new place that day. It was a place on Elm, near the river, a place where no one knew him well. He drank a few beers and played nervously and poorly, dropping forty bucks to a snotty little punk fresh out of high school. He'd spent three hours with a pair of homicide bulls that morning. They'd shown up at his door with a search warrant. A man with swabs had dusted here and there in his closets and his car, had checked his hands and shoes. After a while, when Tony had told them he wanted a lawyer present before he answered any more of their questions, they'd taken what they'd gathered and gone. Tony smiled. They had nothing.

Had they given up on him already? No one seemed to be watching outside the pool room, but he was wary. They'd never trace anything to him, though. He'd gone home from wiring the dynamite to the ignition of Zirbeck's car, used alcohol rub on his fingers and hands, and burned the coveralls and sneakers he'd worn to do the job. Whenever he'd had it in his apartment or his car, the dynamite had been wrapped in several sheets of newspaper. He had left no traces.

He was completely in the clear.

He wondered how Zirbeck was feeling. When he'd first heard the news on his car radio he'd been upset that the cop had escaped, but now he was happier about it. Once or twice, when he was planning the bombing, he'd seen the three of them together, had seen their closeness and envied and hated it. This way Zirbeck had been "fixed" twice as good as killing him would have done. And Zirbeck was a legal cop; Tony knew he wouldn't come looking for him personally.

Not that Tony would have cared. He could take care of himself, but maybe they'd get smart down there and leave him alone now, let him get on with his work.

In his own way Tony believed he was right, jewelry stores had been put on the earth for him to make a living, and those who interfered with him were enemies and deserved to be punished.

He smiled across the table at the kid who was beating him. "Four ball in the corner," he said confidently and made the shot. As he circled the table lining up possibilities, he checked the window. He still didn't see anyone watching the place. After a while, in the manner of the true sociopath, he convinced himself that no one was out there.

The funeral was well attended. Their families were there, and friends from the neighborhood, cops from all over the city and a smattering of curious onlookers drawn by the news stories.

Zirbeck endured it.

When it was done and the closed caskets—one medium-sized, one small—were in the ground, he walked to his car.

Perelli stood by it waiting for him, his very pregnant wife beside him. They were holding hands and Anna Perelli had been crying.

"One day last week," she said, "when Joey was in school, Flora came by to see me. We talked about babies, about taking care of them. I got three brothers and two sisters, and I'm the oldest, but she told me things I didn't know. She—"

"She was a great lady," Perelli finished, drawing Anna closer to him.

Zirbeck nodded. "Yeah, she was. And that Joey was a hell of a kid. I—" He swallowed heavily and rubbed his hand across his face. "Thank you for coming. I guess just about everyone was here."

"Except old Charley Walsh," Perelli said. "You know how much he wanted to be here, Lieutenant, but he's covering Luvisi. I relieve him in a couple of hours." He licked his lips nervously. "We've been watching Luvisi for three days and we're not getting anywhere. He's like a fox, Lieutenant. I thought he'd made me yesterday afternoon, but maybe not. I just drove on and didn't even look at him, and picked him up a minute later. He goes all sorts of places, mostly just drives around. He likes the horse races, he likes the poker games, he shoots some pool. He don't seem worried. Homicide got zilch from him, you know."

"I know, Pete. I read the report. Just stay with him, okay? He'll need money soon. You can always count on that."

Anna Perelli made a sudden grimace of pain.

"He kicked me inside," she said, embarrassed. "He does that a lot."

Zirbeck smiled. "When the baby gets close, Anna, I want to know about it. We'll get someone else to take over for Pete."

"It'll be weeks yet, according to the doctor," she said, resigned to the waiting. "But thank you, Lieutenant. It's good of you to care about us."

Perelli and Anna parked outside their apartment building the next evening and sat there looking at each other.

"How you doing, hon?" he asked her anxiously.

"I'm okay now. The smell of that popcorn just made me feel a little dizzy, but I was okay when I got outside the theater." She shook her head. "I guess I'm tired. You'd be tired too if someone was kicking you in the stomach all day and night."

Perelli stroked her pale cheek lovingly. Anna wasn't strong and the doctor had wondered openly whether she could carry a baby to term, but now she apparently had. He got out of the car and locked his door behind him. On the way around he stuck a matchstick under the hood so he'd know if anyone had opened it when he came back to it in the morning. He opened Anna's door and helped her out and up the steps and into the building.

Their apartment door was ajar. That was wrong. Perelli motioned Anna back and whispered to her, "Go downstairs to Jeff and Sally's and call the precinct." A light was burning behind the open door, though he had switched off the lamps and locked up before they left. He was suddenly afraid, not for himself but for Anna and their unborn child.

"Go," he said again, and she turned obediently and went down the stairs.

When she was out of sight he kicked the door open, keeping himself behind the shield formed by the wall.

Inside there was disaster. Bright red paint had been splashed on the furniture, the carpets, the walls and ceiling. A knife had been taken to everything upholstered. In the kitchen the good dishes had been shattered, the silverware bent into insane shapes. An awful smell came from the oven and he saw that it was turned on. He flipped the dial to off and opened the door: within their everyday plastic dishes smoldered in molten ruins.

Across two walls of the living room someone had scrawled "So long, Mrs. Pete" in crimson paint. On the bedroom walls was a litany of dirty words. The bed had been torn apart, the mattress slashed. Their clothing had been jerked from the closets and dressers and ripped to tatters. Every mirror and picture frame in the apartment had been smashed.

He checked all the rooms, but the intruder was gone.

When he came back out to the hall, Anna was standing in the door with Jeff Tindall, their closest friend in the building.

"I called," she said gravely. "They're sending a car." She began to cry softly.

"You didn't hear anything?" Perelli asked his friend.

Tindall shook his head. "I'm sorry, Pete. We had the TV on all evening."

"Yeah," Perelli said. "Will you take Anna back down to your place? I'll stay here and wait for the squad car."

"Sure, of course. Sally didn't want us coming up here in the first place until you said okay, but Anna insisted. We'll take care of her. You guys can stay with us until—well, you know."

Perelli took Anna's hand. "We'll fix it all, hon. The insurance will pay for everything. We'll fix it up as good as new."

"Yes," she said, but she knew that she would never feel happy there again.

"I'm wondering if I'm right for this job," Perelli told Zirbeck the following morning. "I think he made me and found out who I was, then trashed the apartment to warn me off. Stevick says he was home at the time the vandalism would have had to occur, unless he snuck out the back, which he could easily have done if he'd wanted to." He shook his head. "I think it was him. With only one of us watching him a shift Tony can do things without us knowing it."

Zirbeck waited, nodding now and then.

"With Anna to think about and her not strong, maybe I ought to be out of this, Lieutenant."

"Anybody watching Tony is taking a risk, Pete," Zirbeck said. "But if you'd rather someone else take over I can arrange it."

Perelli winced. "I didn't mean it to sound like it's sounding, Lieutenant."

Zirbeck shrugged. "I can take you off or leave you on, Pete. It's up to you."

Perelli thought about it. He remembered the police photo of the car where Zirbeck's wife and son had died. The car sat in the middle of a wrecked garage, only the burned frame of it having any resemblance to a car anymore. The photograph had affected Perelli then and it was affecting him again now. He thought about Anna and the baby to be, the one she called "he" as if not doubting it would be a boy.

"I guess I'll stay on, Lieutenant."

Zirbeck nodded. "Thanks, Pete," he said.

Lost Tony Luvisi sat outside the jewelry store on Grant Street near the arcade. It had done a brisk business while he was watching, and the merchandise he'd seen in the window when he walked casually past in the late afternoon had been good stuff and not cheap. There was only one clerk on at this time of night, an old man who seemed spry enough but who should be no trouble after Tony cuffed him a time or two.

He'd checked things over carefully. The cop who'd been watching him was no place around. Either he'd shaken him or more likely the jerk had just given up on tailing him and gone home for the night.

The hours on the door of the jewelry store indicated that the place would close at ten, but by nine things had slowed and no one had gone in or out the glass doors for half an hour. Tony could see the old man doing something behind the counter, cleaning it.

He got out a ski mask from his pocket. He'd bought a dozen of them at a bargain store while driving through another city months ago. He kept them hidden in an abandoned house near where he lived, visiting the place at night to pick up a new one for each job. The old ones he burned after use. The newspapers had called him the ski-mask robber, and one reporter, more acute than the others, had noticed how the description of the ski mask used varied from robbery to robbery.

Tony needed money. At nine-thirty he paused at the corner of the jewelry store, inspecting the area one more time, a careful workman. Satisfied, he put on the ski mask. He went inside.

As the ski-masked figure disappeared through the door Pete Perelli got out of the truck he'd borrowed from an obliging neighbor that afternoon, worried that Lost Tony had made his car by now. Perelli went after him. He wished there was time to call for backup, but there was no radio in the truck and of course he couldn't go looking for a phone booth, not now.

Tony slapped the old man. "Open the safe or you're dead, pops." He slapped him again and the old man whimpered.

Tony felt more than saw the front door swing open and he turned to it with an angry snarl. The man who came through the door was a cop, the one with the pregnant wife. He wore an ugly leisure suit they'd have laughed at in some of the places Tony frequented, but he was carrying a gun in his right hand. They wouldn't have laughed at the gun. Tony snapped a shot at him, which took glass out of a display window, and fled for the back. When he'd cased the place he'd seen a back door and knew it opened from the inside, but not the outside. He went through it at a run and pounded down the asphalt alley behind the store. The corner was fifty feet away.

Behind him he heard a yelled warning, then a shot. He increased his speed and turned slightly to fire again as he ran.

He never heard Perelli's second shot. The bullet caught him in a line with his right eye and took out the front of his skull. He was dead before he hit the ground.

There were half a dozen of them in Zirbeck's office and Perelli haltingly told the story once more.

"It was dark and he was a moving target, but I should have gotten him in the leg." He shook his head. "I was running and the gun just wasn't steady." He scowled, thinking about it. "I was trying to get him in the leg, but it was dark and he had a gun."

"It's okay, Pete," Zirbeck said. "He'd already fired at you once. When you hit him he was apparently turning to get off another shot."

Perelli frowned. "Maybe I wanted it to end the way it

ended. He got your wife and boy and he broke into my place and tore it up good, scared the hell out of me and Anna." He looked down at his feet.

Zirbeck gave a nod and the other men saw it. In turn each of them patted Perelli on the shoulder and left the room. In moments there were only Zirbeck and Perelli left.

"You go home and you forget about Tony Luvisi," Zirbeck ordered. "Take Anna out and buy her a nice dinner and some wine and then go home and get some sleep."

"Maybe I meant to kill him," Perelli said. "Maybe I never gave him a chance."

"Not you, Pete. You're the best I've got. That's why I wanted you on this job." He shook Perelli's hand.

Perelli forced a smile. "You sure?"

"I'm sure," Zirbeck said. "Now go home."

Perelli went out of the room with his head up.

Zirbeck sat behind his desk. He remembered that day in the bedroom, only a week ago now though it felt like months. He remembered the feel of the gun in his hands, remembered wanting to use it on Tony Luvisi, remembered knowing he couldn't ever murder in cold, calculating blood.

He'd thought Perelli could do it, though. Perelli had a toughness that Zirbeck had never seen in another man. He was soft and gentle with his wife, with his friends, but tough with the evil world that lay so close, so near. He acted instinctively and that made him, in many ways, a good cop. And especially a good choice for the Luvisi case.

It had sickened Zirbeck to vandalize the Perellis' apartment as he had, to write those threats on the walls and terrify poor innocent Anna.

But Lost Tony was dead now, and Flora and Joey could, in Zirbeck's mind, sleep.

And that, Zirbeck thought, was all that mattered.

The Home

Shelby's second heart attack came during a trial in which he was defending a man named Blandon on a jewel burglary. He remembered the crushing pain, falling, then blackness.

When he was allowed to leave the hospital, it was only upon his promise to move to a nursing home.

Shelby sold his condo and appointed his bank to handle his affairs.

He then prepared to die. He found that it took very little effort and was, except for recurring dark-of-the-night sweats when he was sure he'd not live to see morning again, boring.

He was sixty-seven and he still seemed healthy enough after he'd recovered from the attack. There was angina pain and shortness of breath, but that was it as far as overt symptoms went. His doctor explained to him that his heart was *insufficient* and that he needed a place where he could have constant medical attention available. So, a nursing home.

At times, thinking about his bad heart made Shelby smile. There were lawyers, particularly criminal prosecutors, who'd have sworn on a pile of religious tracts that he was heartless, lawyers he'd crushed by cleverness in closing argument or by vicious cross-examination of unsure prosecution witnesses. He'd mostly defended persons accused of murder, but he'd taken other criminal cases when there were no murder cases to be tried. He'd been an advocate's advocate. He'd taken only cases where he believed the accused innocent, losing some, winning a lot.

He'd been the best, but now there'd be no more trials. His heart condition made it impossible. The tension of a trial, the open warfare wherein a client might lose his freedom or life, had been what he lived for. Without the courtroom he felt useless. *And old—finally old.*

The nursing home was named Eden. It sat on a hill in the middle of wooded acreage ten miles distant from the city where Shelby had practiced. It had been a private estate, but when it had been sold for a nursing home the mansion had been modernized. There was a high, barbed fence around the property and an armed guard at the closed gate. *Safe.*

There was a separate building near the gate for visitors, but visitors seldom came. Eden specialized in patients who didn't have close relatives. The literature given to those interested in the home was frank about it. "We want people who need us. We want to be your family."

Shelby had selected the place after reading various competing tracts and then had been interviewed by Mr. Hoskins from the home before being "accepted."

"Ours is a quiet place," Mr. Hoskins had warned. "We control all visitation. We also don't permit our patients to travel outside the nursing home. We have our own inhouse medical staff and we would expect your doctor to turn your complete medical file over to our people. Our staff is the best in the field of geriatric medicine. Would anything I've said be a problem? If so, we can stop now."

"I doubt it," Shelby said. His own doctor didn't like him. The doctor's house had been burglarized once and he'd told Shelby tartly he had no use for lawyers who protected criminals.

Mr. Hoskins looked approvingly at Shelby's written application. "I see you list no family. Understand again that we limit visitation to once every other week with relatives. All visitation is carried out in an area adjacent to the home under strict supervision. We can't have visitors upsetting our patients."

Shelby shook his head. "I've two cousins, but I've not heard from either of them in years. I never married. Never found the time. There'd be no visitors."

"You were a lawyer. Were you with a large firm?"

"Single practitioner," Shelby said. "I was ordered to shut my office down after my last attack."

"You seem to have the necessary finances to pay us," Hoskins continued, his tone favorable.

"Yes," Shelby said. "I can pay you. Your place isn't as expensive as many. Yet, except for your visitation rules, it seems the best. How do you manage that?"

"We're privately endowed. Certain of our patients have left us their estates or a part of their estates as a reward for the care we gave them in their declining years. That's why we're careful about admissions." Mr. Hoskins smiled a little. "During your stay with us, if you find our facilities satisfactory, we would expect you to consider a gift to the home upon your eventual demise."

"Is that required?" Shelby asked, not liking that part.

"Certainly not," Hoskins answered reprovingly. "But you should remember that your care is being partially paid for by those who resided at the home before you. We ask only that you consider such a bequest once you've experienced the care we provide."

It sounded reasonable. Shelby examined Hoskins. The nursing-home administrator seemed above reproach. His clothes were expensive and neat, he was fiftyish, and he wore hornrims. All his movements were precise. A jury would believe him. He vaguely reminded Shelby of a child molester he had defended (and lost) years back. Very proper.

They shook hands and it was settled. Shelby signed a penalty-clause contract.

Mr. Hoskins smiled as he was leaving. "We'll see you soon," he said. "Have a good day."

And so Shelby moved to Eden.

The first patient he met was a onetime client. His name was Julian Kay and Shelby had defended him twenty years back when Kay's wife had died under suspicious but ultimately unprovable (at least as far as Kay was concerned) circumstances. Arsenic poisoning. The State's difficulties had been in showing that Kay had administered the poison to his wife when tests ordered by Shelby showed Kay himself had traces of arsenic in his own body. Shelby knew that those who used arsenic as a poison often managed to accidentally ingest some of it themselves. He suspected Kay's wife had tried to poison Kay and botched it. That was his winning trial tactic.

Kay had the next room. He sat upright in bed. "How are you?" Shelby asked solicitously when Hoskins introduced them.

Kay ignored the question. He watched Shelby. "Devil," he said. "Devil!" He shook with agitation.

Hoskins drew Shelby away. "He makes no sense some days. He's had a series of small strokes. He's been here for a long time."

"How long?"

Hoskins made a vague gesture. "A long time. Years. Why do you ask?"

Shelby shrugged. He'd lost track of Kay soon after the trial. The man had been peculiar. But he'd sworn his innocence and Shelby had believed him.

At times thereafter Shelby would nod in at Kay from the door without receiving a response. Kay's color was bad and he was about fifty pounds lighter than Shelby remembered him. Shelby heard one of the pretty nurses say Kay was "on his deathbed." Sometimes Shelby could hear him groaning at night. He also heard doctors in the room working on Kay and saw attendants pushing complicated life-support machines into his room. But Kay lived on.

There were things Shelby didn't agree with in the home's routine. The food was good enough, but it wasn't a coronary diet. It was high-fat food—meat and gravy, and rich desserts at noon and at night. For breakfast it was eggs with bacon or sausage, heavily buttered toast, pancakes, and sweet rolls, served leisurely and late. It was the kind of food Shelby had wanted but not allowed himself to eat outside, after the first attack. (Meals were served on china with heavy silverware, a budding rose in a vase on the bed tray, by a smiling attendant—female and pretty for the male patients, handsome and muscular for the female patients.)

The doctor assigned to Shelby, Dr. Cart, seemed vaguely familiar to him. Shelby asked him about the diet and he spoke of "good" triglycerides and cholesterol and "bad" ones, and of a secret Eden food-treatment formula. He took Shelby's pulse and listened intently to the faulty heart. "You're doing well," he said. He then marked a special diet for him on his card, which he told Shelby was optional if a patient worried about his diet and requested another.

"We're all born with ailing hearts," he joked. "It stops, we stop. Sleep. Watch TV. See what a fine set you have? Trust us. Relax."

Shelby nodded, thinking the humor unfunny, at least to a man with a heart as "insufficient" as his.

Thereafter, sometimes the special diet came, sometimes it didn't. When it did come, it was unappetizing, as if the fine Eden cooks had thrown it on the plate in disgust. He didn't complain again about the food, and gradually the regular diet returned to full-time status.

Shelby did feel well, but he'd felt that way before both heart attacks. He slept nine or ten hours a night. He tried to keep from gaining weight by eating sparsely. He looked in vain for any sort of exercise facility to burn up calories and keep his aging muscles fit.

"Don't you have exercise facilities here?" he asked the doctor.

Dr. Cart sniffed. "No. We decided against an exercise area. We believe that our patients benefit more from rest than exercise. You're not a boy anymore, Mr. Shelby. You'll live longer doing things our way."

"But surely some mild exercise should be beneficial?"

"I'm not in total disagreement," Dr. Cart conceded. "You're a bit younger than our usual patient. I'll allow you to improvise."

Shelby improvised and walked. If there was angina pain or shortness of breath he stopped for a while, then walked some more.

He observed that a high percentage of the patients at Eden ran from mildly fat to clearly obese. When he commented on it, Dr. Cart frowned. "You were a lawyer outside, Mr. Shelby, not a doctor. Leave the practice of medicine to us. Fat isn't automatically fatal."

There was a decent library, which kept Shelby from becoming a TV addict like so many of the other patients.

When fall became winter, more of the walks he took were confined to inside the mansion. He was allowed to roam everywhere except the staff areas. The staff door was kept locked, but now and then when the door was open he caught a glimpse of rich draperies, lush furniture, and a hanging chandelier. Shelby guessed those rooms had been the central part of the original mansion. Some nights he heard sounds of revelry from within. Early in the morning he could hear the staff breakfasting together before the patients were served.

The kitchen, the surgery, and the intensive-care rooms were also in that area and out of bounds. Once, during an evening walk, he examined the lock on the staff door. It was a simple one. Blandon, the accused burglar and jewel thief Shelby had last represented, had taught him about locks, after convincing Shelby he was innocent "this time." Shelby thought he could open the staff lock given the time plus some tools in his manicure set and wallet.

The home was becoming an easy life. Late breakfast, noon lunch, early dinner. Read, sleep, and walk. Outside, snow fell. Christmas and New Year's came. The staff held a sedate party for the patients and a wild one for themselves behind the staff door.

Shelby counted staff—doctors, nurses, attendants, maintenance people. There were a great many. None seemed to work very hard. Several times Shelby could have sworn he smelled scotch on Cart's breath. And the night attendant in Shelby's area seemed to sleep better than Shelby.

Eden had a sixty-patient capacity. Multiplying what he paid for his own care times sixty did not add to a figure Shelby found impressive as revenue. The remainder must come from endowments.

The home was extremely quiet. Shelby saw the doctors, nurses, and attendants doling out pills for nerves, for sleep, for everything—pills and smiles—and decided it was quiet because so many of the old people were heavily doped. It was a great place to eat and sleep and die.

But what if you weren't ready to die?

One night, out of boredom, he tested his burglar-client's instructions and picked open the lock of one of the medicine chests, using a sharp cuticle pick from his manicure set. He managed it silently and easily in the darkness while the night attendant snored. The chest was stocked with tranquilizers and sedatives. A locked compartment inside yielded to further probing. There were things he didn't recognize. Some of the bottles were marked with skull and crossbones. Others were strong sedatives or narcotics. Bottles of both types had been opened. Shelby didn't think that unusual. He knew doctors used all sorts of medicines and that some poisons did not kill if given in careful doses. He closed the chest back up.

He'd always been a light sleeper, but now he found himself sleeping well and long. Maybe there was something in the cocoa. It was oversweet, full of whipped cream, and had a slightly metallic aftertaste. At first he drank it, but later he poured it into a large flowerpot beside his bed. Then he would prowl Eden's dark halls until dawn. He was restless and, for the first time in his life, lonely.

Hoskins, the administrator, talked with him in his office one day. By that time Shelby had made a few acquaintances. There was a fat old man he played chess with. The man had suffered a stroke and lost most of his ability to speak and all movement on his right side, but he could still use his left hand to move chessmen. He was an expert player. They kept the old man, whose name was Detmen, heavily tranquilized, but Detmen seemed resistant to the medicine and could function around it. Most of the people in the home were lumps. Detmen was refreshing.

His movements with the left hand were quick and snakelike. "Gotchee," he'd say. "Checkmay." Then he'd grin lopsidedly. A fine old man who'd been an architect.

Detmen didn't like Dr. Cart. "Dite duck," he'd mutter darkly when Cart was near. Shelby finally figured that he was trying to say, "Diet doc."

There were three elderly ladies who invited Shelby to play bridge. They painted their lips and flirted with him outrageously, tittering at each other behind their cards. He was gallant with them and tried not to trump their aces. Then one of them, Laura Shannon, died one night and that ended the bridge sessions. The two survivors seemed not to know each other afterward. Shelby th ght they might be getting added doses of tranquilizer from their doctors. Or maybe Laura Shannon had been the glue that held the bridge games together.

He asked Dr. Cart about it. "What did Laura Shannon die of?"

Cart pursed his lips. "She had many problems. High blood pressure, a bad heart, and diabetes. She was over eighty. People don't live forever, Mr. Shelby."

"She was the most active of all the bridge players," Shelby said. "She seemed perfectly all right to me."

"Maybe hyperactivity helped speed her death," Dr. Cart answered reasonably. "That's something you might think about, Mr. Shelby. Are you walking too much? Are you too busy? Our attendants say you wander around a great deal, even at night."

"I'm restless," Shelby explained. "I need the exercise."

Detmen died as Shelby started his fifth month in the home. It was during an in-home operation Cart told Shelby had been intended to open up the large artery running from the heart to the brain. Detmen had said nothing to Shelby about any operation.

No more chess or bridge. Just walking.

Sometimes he caught the attendants watching him as he prowled the darkened halls. Sometimes he thought they used care in what they said to him and how.

I'm paranoid, he thought.

With the two people he'd liked most at Eden dead, Shelby tried to watch the soaps during the day but couldn't stand them. Instead, he watched the snow beyond his window and dreamed of green grass and outdoor walks.

Hoskins smiled, interrupting Shelby's walk, and led him to his office.

"Are you enjoying your life here, Mr. Shelby?"

"It's adequate," Shelby said.

"No more than that?" Hoskins asked, pouting a little.

Shelby relented. "It's nice." He tried a bit of sarcasm. "Very quiet. It's hard to become acquainted with people. They die."

Hoskins nodded piously. "Death is only a part of life. We must all face it sooner or later. This is a home for old, sick people. We keep them alive and happy as long as we can."

"Yes." Shelby had been thinking a great deal about Detmen. "But Mr. Detmen might have lived if he hadn't been operated on."

Hoskins shrugged. "He wanted to be better, to be well again. Unfortunately, it wasn't to be. He died on the operating table. It was a shame." He leaned forward. "May I talk with you on something of importance?"

Shelby nodded assent.

"We've had our lawyers prepare our form will plus a codicil to an already existing will showing bequests to Eden. The bequest figure in the forms is what we recommend to someone in your financial bracket without close relatives. Of course, you can devise any figure you want, less or more. We'd like you to examine the forms."

Shelby said all right.

Hoskins handed him a sheaf of papers and shook his hand moistly. "May I call on you in a week or so?"

"You said there was no obligation?"

"Absolutely." Mr. Hoskins smiled. He reminded Shelby of a minister he'd defended for the murder of his sister, a man who swore on a Bible he had not done the murder.

Shelby had dressed him all in black and had him carry and read his Bible in court while the trial proceeded. The jury had come back in an hour with a verdict of not guilty.

Shelby took the will back to his room, examined it, and shoved it in a drawer. His own will was made. His money was to be shared by a youth club he admired and his university. He saw no reason to change it.

He told Hoskins his decision a week later. The man inclined his head. "Perhaps you'll change your mind as time passes," he said. "Some do. I hope you'll continue to consider it."

Shelby found himself watching what went on around him more closely. Having made it known that he would leave the home no money in his will, he wondered what would happen.

The food and service remained good. But he realized that someone shadowed him those nights he walked the darkened halls. And it seemed even harder to stay awake now than before he had started to dump the hot chocolate.

No one came to visit, but although Shelby expected no one a fragile hope remained. He had a few legal friends outside. One might come. His secretary of many years had moved to Florida when the office closed. He asked about calling out to his bank and was refused. When he insisted, Dr. Cart came to see him.

"We don't let you do that," he said. "You're here because you ruined your health with worry and work. Now we take care of all that for you. Every month we send an itemized bill to your bank, along with a statement of your physical condition." He shook his head and again Shelby caught a faint odor of scotch. "Relax. Use the home. Enjoy us."

"I only want to talk to the trust officer to see how things are going," Shelby said. "Is this a nursing home or a prison?"

"It's a nursing home, with our own highly successful methods. We insist that our rules be followed. Reread your contract with us, Mr. Shelby." Dr. Cart stood for a moment, lost in thought. *"Write* your bank. That should be good therapy for you."

"Speaking of therapy, aren't there any trips outside?" Shelby asked. "I've got cabin fever." He couldn't admit he was lonely.

Cart shook his head. "We used to do trips, but we stopped. They were very traumatic for the patients. One man died on the bus and we had sheriffs and investigators all over us for days. It was very upsetting for us and the patients."

Shelby studied him. He remembered what Detmen had said. "Dite duck." And he remembered something else, something he'd read long ago in the newspapers about a doctor who'd specialized in quick-weight-loss diets, who'd given speed pills by the bucketful to his patients. Shelby remembered the scandal and the trial, but only vaguely. Had Cart's license been revoked?

"Before he died, Mr. Detmen said that you used to specialize in diet therapy, Dr. Cart. Is that true?"

Cart smiled coldly. "I came into the field of geriatrics some years ago when I decided to change my specialty." He examined Shelby with clinical eyes. "I'm reputed to be quite good in my new area of interest."

"I see," Shelby said. "But did you specialize in diets at one time?"

The doctor looked back at him without answering.

"I only asked," Shelby said softly . . .

For the first time Shelby had second thoughts about Eden. His fear of death had abated and what came to him in his first moments of suspicion was not renewed fear but anger. Could this place be some kind of trap for old people without close family or friends? Did they cage the unwary, get them to change their wills, then kill them with poor care or a pill? Or on an operating table, like tough old Detmen?

Thinking about it at length made the idea seem preposterous, but he continued to think about it anyway. Eden would be a perfect place to pull off such a scheme. What few visitors came would have little interest in the patients' concerns. Shelby knew better than most that the world was imperfect. He knew a hundred confidence schemes and how they were run.

He considered his situation. It would be profitless for them to kill him unless he changed his will in their favor. Then one day he saw Hoskins enter Kay's room and shut the door. Hearing him leave a short while later, he decided he would pay a visit to Kay himself that night.

He waited until late, until the night attendant had gone for coffee, and then entered the room next door. Kay's old eyes followed him from door to bed. Lost eyes.

"Do you remember me?" Shelby asked.

Nothing.

"I defended you once in court."

After a moment there was a tiny look of recognition. Kay nodded. "You defended me, devil."

When Kay said no more, Shelby opened the bedside table drawer. It was empty except for a sheaf of papers like those Shelby had received from Hoskins, legal papers concerning new wills and codicils to old ones. "Did you sign those papers for the home?"

"Today," Kay whispered. "I wanted it done." He turned his face away from Shelby and pulled the pillow closer to his head. "I killed her all those years ago," he said softly to the wall. "But the jury said I didn't kill her. You did that, devil."

"And now the staff here is going to let you die, is that it?" Shelby asked. "To reward you? Because you want that?"

Kay watched the wall without answering.

From far away there was a sound. Shelby left the room.

He was now fairly sure Eden was a murder trap, but there still seemed to be a reasonable doubt. He'd lived by reasonable doubt. Even if they let Kay die, that didn't make it certain they were killing others.

But there was enough evidence for Shelby to want out. There were other nursing homes. He sat on his bed and tried to figure a way of escaping Eden. He couldn't climb the fence or get out the guarded gate. Maybe he could hide in the backseat of a doctor's car. But he remembered seeing the guards looking in the backseats of departing cars. It had puzzled him until now. Then he had a thought. What about the letter Cart had suggested?

Shelby wrote a long, devious letter to his bank and delivered it to Dr. Cart. The letter asked that the bank send someone to the nursing home to see Shelby. He made the letter insistent and specified that they send a lawyer he'd known, making the lawyer seem to be a bank employee.

That was the day Kay died.

No one came to visit Shelby on the week that followed, or the one following that. One morning into the third week, while Shelby was preparing a new, more strident letter, something went wrong. Nausea and blackness. Dr. Cart was summoned quickly and Shelby's bed was pushed down the hall, through the staff door, and into an intensive-care room. Shelby felt no pain, only a loss of seeing and being. He was hooked to monitoring devices. Dr. Cart gave him several injections and took his pulse and blood pressure. A nurse stood watch.

Inside Shelby's brain, when he could get around the drugs, he discovered anger.

If he lived—

He thought he might live. He could perceive them working feverishly, presumably toward that purpose.

He wandered away from consciousness.

Waking was difficult. It was hard to open his eyes, so he kept them closed.

There was no pain in his chest and his heartbeat seemed to be regular.

He could hear bits of conversation. He thought one voice was Dr. Cart's, soft but authoritative. He seemed to be in another room. "He does enough sedatives, that doesn't solve our problems."

"Codicil—" That was Mr. Hoskins' unctuous voice.

"He won't do—" Yes, it was definitely Dr. Cart, but his words were difficult to make out.

"Who would hear? We can always give shock treatments if we have to."

"True. Perhaps we'll try. He'll be grateful we saved his life. But he's been a problem—always nosing around."

"He has money," Hoskins said firmly. "You know our kind of patient isn't easy to find."

Shelby's sick heart pounded alarmingly. There was no longer a reasonable doubt.

When he finally opened his eyes, a pretty nurse smiled at him with foxlike eyes. He remembered how to influence jurors and he smiled back.

"I'm alive," he said, as if amazed about it. "You've saved my life." His voice sounded shockingly weak.

The nurse smiled down at him and he reminded himself all of them were in on it. It couldn't work any other way. A whole staff of murderers. Forced bequests and sudden death for the contented, TV-addicted ancients, the good life for the staff.

Back in his room, he tried to get up, but his legs were

gone. He was afraid of the food, but he ate it stoically. If it was drugged, there was no indication. He talked the nurse into bringing him a portable wheelchair.

He smiled at Cart and Hoskins and the rest of the staff. He was effusively grateful to them. He asked Hoskins for a new codicil form to study. He tried to appear weaker than he was and the eyes that had carefully watched him temporarily relaxed. He'd bought a little time.

When Hoskins visited again (with the codicil form), Shelby said: "I'll fill in a figure for you very soon. Give me a few days."

Two nights later he returned to the drug chest when the attendant was asleep. He opened both locks. A long life of cross-examining pathologists and lab technicians had made him aware of the power of some of the numbing and deadly things. Those with skull and crossbones in the chest he took on trust. Good enough for them, good enough for him.

A night attendant seeking clean linen almost caught him as he wheeled on toward the staff area, but he made it safely to the door and picked the lock with the manicure tool and a plastic credit card slipped down to hold open the lock. He rolled his chair inside and found the kitchen area.

He dumped only light sedatives into the steaming coffee urn, trusting it would make the early coffee drinkers sleepy as they awaited the main course. He then used the poisons, tasting or smelling each additive gingerly and discarding any that were too bitter or too pungent. The pills he ground to a fine powder. Moving around slowly and with great care, he found a huge bowl of beaten eggs in the refrigerator and added a combination of the poisons. He put some of the poison in the freshly squeezed orange juice and more in the milk. There was a dispenser for mineral water at the end of a service table. There he was moderate, careful not to alter the color.

The staff would breakfast and then they would serve the late-rising patients. *If they could.*

A doctor might detect the poisons, but Shelby wondered if detection would be enough to save them all. Or many of them. He hoped not.

There would be sheriffs and state police, sirens and flashing lights. *Lovely.* Perhaps he'd be accused. Maybe he could conduct his own case. Cinch self-defense.

He rolled unseen back to his bed and napped for a time. Something in the drugs he'd tasted made his heart fibrillate wildly for a time, but it passed. He felt weak, but well enough when he got up a few hours later. When Mr. Hoskins came in the outside door, just before the staff breakfast hour, Shelby was there to meet him. He reached into a pocket of the chair cover and offered over the codicil.

"This is what I want," Shelby told the administrator. "If you'll bring two witnesses along sometime today I'll sign it." He started to turn away, then stopped. "Anytime after breakfast, but before *General Hospital.*"

Mr. Hoskins beamed when he read the figure Shelby had inserted.

"Have a good day," Shelby told him, moving off in the direction of his room.

Searcher

Cannert lay ill on the couch in his recently rented apartment. Through the big window, he could see Davisson's modest house with its attached garage. The garage door was up, and the red pickup truck was gone.

Cannert considered checking the house again, if and when he felt better, but he'd found nothing before and he doubted anything had changed. Davisson was as wary as a fox and might have detected the last entry. He could be watching and waiting for another. The police had jailed Davisson but were unable to hold him. Cannert sighed and continued to watch.

The doctor came. He checked Cannert over with expert fingers.

"I seldom make house calls," he said, smiling down at Cannert. "Doctors don't have to in Florida, but you interest me. You're sick, but you refuse to go to the hospital or come to my office. I ask myself why. How long did your people up north give you?"

"A year at the outside. That was more than seven months ago."

The doctor nodded soothingly. "Maybe you've got a bit more time than that. You're not swollen. I see no radical changes. Sometimes there are small remissions." He shook his head. "I'm not promising you a thing, but it could be. I think you're nauseous because you're not eating right. What have you had today?"

Cannert told him. The list was short.

The doctor scribbled out a prescription. "Take these before meals, and try to eat regularly. Stay away from fried and high-fat foods." He looked sternly down at Cannert. "And come in the next time you need me. I'd like to do some X rays." He searched through his case and handed Cannert a bottle of large tablets. "These are nonprescription. Chew up one or two with half a glass of water when you feel nauseous. They're only flavored chalk, but they'll help. You can buy more in any drugstore."

"Thanks, Doctor," Cannert said humbly.

When the doctor had gone, Cannert managed to get up. He felt weak and his stomach churned, but he found he could walk. He went to the tiny kitchen, got a glass of water, and chewed one of the big tablets. It tasted sweet and chalky. In a while he felt better.

He drove to a drugstore and got the new prescription filled. He took one of the new capsules, added a pain pill, and then ate a ham sandwich at the drugstore lunch counter. By the time he was finished, he felt much better.

He listened to the chatter of the ancients around him. Centralia was an old folks' town, inland from the warm sea, cheaper than the ocean cities. People vacationed and moved here to sit vacant-eyed in the sun, to play golf and shuffleboard—perhaps, eventually, to die.

Cannert thought it was the kind of town Martha would have liked.

In the newspapers he had scanned in his travels, Cannert had read reports indicating that a lot of old people had disappeared from Centralia. A later story mentioned that a Lieutenant Ryan was in charge of the missing persons cases, and that an Alfred Davisson had been picked up for questioning and later released.

So Cannert had come to Centralia looking for clues to the whereabouts of Martha, his wife, who'd traveled to

Florida seeking a place for them, then vanished. Centralia was somewhere to look while time ran on out. *Keeping busy.*

At five that afternoon, Cannert walked into the Precinct Bar and Grill, across the street from the police station. He took a seat at the far end of the bar, ordered a Canadian and water, tipped adequately but not munificently, and waited. He'd been in the place twice before, and a few regulars gave him tentative nods. He nodded back.

Ryan sat three seats down from him. Cannert ignored the man for the moment. Another bar regular, a red-nosed patrolman who didn't like Ryan, had told him about Ryan's problems. Drinking had cost him his wife and probably any chance for further advancement as a policeman.

Six o'clock came. Much of the bar crowd had moved on. A few couples came in and took booths before ordering drinks and dinner. Cannert motioned to the bartender. "See if I might buy Lieutenant Ryan a drink," he said.

Ryan looked up at him curiously and nodded. Cannert walked over and took an adjoining stool.

"I still do a little free-lancing for some papers up north. I'm down here on vacation, and I've read about all your missing people. I thought it might make a story. How many are missing?"

"No one's sure. Twenty. Maybe more. Old people flit in and out of Centralia like summer moths. Some I think are missing probably aren't. Some I don't list as missing maybe are."

He sipped the drink Cannert had bought him. "I doubt I could do you any good. We had a guy we watched and then picked up, but nothing came of it. Alfred Davisson. He's a bug. He was seen with a couple of people who later turned up missing." Ryan smiled without humor. "When his lawyer got him out, Davisson sued me for false arrest. Then he sued me and the town again because we kept watching him. The local powers didn't like that, or me for causing it. I got told to stop. So I stopped. Guys like Davisson should die hard, but I guess they won't in today's world."

"You're pretty sure he was involved?"

Ryan shrugged. "Maybe."

"You said he was a bug. What does that mean?"

"It means he's wacky. His elevator doesn't go to the top floor. If we let Davisson do the deciding, retired old people wouldn't come here to Centralia. He wants building stopped—and no more roads. But mostly, no more people. He files lawsuits against anything and everything. He's a great law man." Ryan grinned. "He ain't popular. But he has a following of sorts. Other kooks."

"What's he do for a living?" Cannert asked.

"Works at the biscuit place. He's the head man. Good enough job, I'd guess. Better than mine." He peered into his drink as if seeking answers there. "They don't work no more than six or eight people out there these days. Everything's automated." He looked Cannert over carefully. "You kind of look like a bug, too."

"How's that?"

"Too thin and tired. Your eyes are old. Did you maybe used to be a cop?"

"No. It could be newspaper reporting is the same kind of thing," Cannert said, not liking the man's acuteness.

"Maybe so," Ryan said, losing interest. He looked down at his almost empty glass. "I had a hunch on Davisson. I did the natural thing. I picked him up. He called his lawyers, and the town and I got sued. Nuisance stuff, but the people I work for don't like nuisances." He tapped Cannert on the arm. "So I don't like Davisson." He tinkled his ice impatiently.

Cannert nodded again to the bartender.

The "biscuit place" turned out to be a dog biscuit factory. Cannert drove his Ford past it the next afternoon. It sat aloofly behind a high fence on a large lot at the edge of town. A bored, uniformed guard stood at the wide front gate. Davisson's red pickup truck was one of about half a dozen vehicles parked in a small lot.

The building was long and gray. The only windows Cannert saw were near the top. A single door opened from the parking area. A well-painted sign on one side of the structure read: "Bowser's Bone Food—For Discriminating Dogs."

Cannert drove on around, taking a graveled, tree-lined road. On the far side of the building, he could see a loading dock. A few men worked there, piling cartons into trucks.

As Cannert watched from concealment, two more big trucks entered the grounds. The driver of the first one got out, nodded a greeting to the men working on the dock, and pressed a button on a shiny pole. A large metal cover lifted smoothly from the ground. He reentered his cab and backed up to the hole which had been exposed. Stepping down once more, he removed chains and a tarpaulin from the vehicle's rear.

Cannert saw animal carcasses that looked freshly killed. He thought some of them were cattle, some hogs. The man attached ropes and hooks to the carcasses. They were lifted from the truck and then lowered into the hole. When the first vehicle was unloaded, the second one backed in. This time the cargo was grain of some kind.

Davisson came out and stood overseeing the operations from a raised area on the loading dock. Cannert watched him through binoculars and felt the hair along the back of his neck rise, his blood run faster. This could be the man who'd gotten Martha. Cannert felt it was. Martha's last card had come from not very far away.

Davisson was strongly built, maybe late forties or early fifties, balding. His eyes were cruel and shifty.

Cannert stayed out of sight and observed the proceedings throughout the long, hot afternoon. At five, the other men left, but Davisson remained. At seven, Davisson came out, got in his pickup, and maneuvered it to the gate. He unlocked the gate, drove through, then locked it again. Cannert watched him leave but continued waiting. In a while, the red pickup came back past the plant, slowed, then moved on after Davisson had taken a long look. *A wary fox,* Cannert thought again.

Cannert extracted the little Hy Hunter Derringer .38 from his Ford's glove compartment and walked along the back fence of the plant. He found he was trembly and ill again, so he chewed two more of the big white tablets. They helped, even without water.

Halfway along the fence, there was a place where heavy rainstorms had cut a depression beneath it. A large man couldn't have squeezed under, but Cannert managed easily.

The doors along the loading dock were secured, and so was the front entrance. The windows were too high to allow easy entry. Cannert prowled on, then remembered the deliveries of the afternoon.

He found and pressed the button on the pole and watched the cover lift slowly from the ground. He clambered down the rungs of a metal ladder into the murky interior of the exposed cavity before stopping to let his eyes adjust to the deeper darkness. On this subterranean level, he found an inner door that opened off into an area beneath the gray building. He pushed through.

There was a strong smell of dead animals and feed grains. Cannert felt his way along a dusty corridor, found some stairs, and went up. On the floor above, the air was cooler. He moved past complex machines and huge vats, some of them bubbling with heat. Relays clicked on and off. Motors whirred softly. Cannert inspected it all, taking his time.

At the front of the building, he discovered what he soon decided was Davisson's office. It lay behind a sturdy, but unlocked, steel door. Inside, there was an impressive array of panels, switches, and complicated gauges, with red and green lights blinking at the bidding of a nearby computer.

In the half light, Cannert found Davisson's desk and chair. Papers were strewn about the top. When Cannert held them closer to the red and green lights, he found that all of them were business letters or order forms. He put them back where they'd been.

The desk drawers were locked. It seemed like a dead end. Cannert headed for the door and then turned to take a last look. In one corner a heavy wooden chair, worn and scarred, caught his eye. It was the room's only additional seating. Cannert walked over and explored it with his fingers, discovering a small opening between chair seat and chair bottom. An idea and a hunch came at the same time.

He took the derringer out of his pocket and pushed it into the recess. It fit snugly, out of sight. He considered the situation carefully, finally deciding to leave it there. If he was wrong about Davisson, losing the gun was a small price to pay. But if he was right, the hidden weapon could be invaluable.

He left the plant as he'd entered it, closing the metal cover behind him.

For nine days, Cannert kept watch on the factory and on Davisson's house. Several times, at the house, people came and went. Once, some kind of meeting was held. A tall man in a black coat gave some kind of blessing to begin it. People got up and talked heatedly while Davisson nodded in agreement from a front table. At one point, bumper stickers were passed out. Cannert later saw Davisson attach one to his truck. It read: "Florida for Floridians—Others Stay Out."

Cannert felt good again. His appetite returned as he maintained his vigil.

On the tenth night, something happened which Cannert had been expecting. He saw Davisson turn out his lights and slip from the house. He was carrying a package.

Cannert got to his own vehicle as quickly as he could, panting a little, tired by the time he arrived. He waited until he saw Davisson's pickup exit his driveway, then followed as Davisson drove to the main highway, toward the biscuit plant. Seizing an opportunity, Cannert passed the red truck, cutting Davisson off. Hearing the pickup's horn blare angrily, he raised a placating hand, wanting to be noticed.

When he was five hundred yards ahead, Cannert pulled off the road and popped his hood release. He got out and stood beside the apparently disabled car.

The truck's lights picked him up. Cannert knew Davisson was seeing Illinois plates and the wasted old body of an "outsider."

The red pickup sped on past. Cannert felt his heart slow as the gamble failed. Then, at the next crossroads, he saw brake lights come on. The truck made a U-turn, then another, before it stopped behind Cannert's Ford. Davisson got out.

"Problems?" he asked politely.

"Guess this car's just getting old, like me," Cannert responded. "I passed you and it just quit. Fate maybe. Could I get you to drop me at a service station?"

"Sure," Davisson answered easily. He smiled, but the smile never touched his eyes. The man was even larger up close than at a distance. Formidable.

Cannert climbed into the cab of the red truck.

"New around here?" Davisson asked.

"Just moved into Centralia a few weeks back. No relatives left. I needed to find someplace warm. Sure is that here. And it's less expensive than the ocean cities. I guess I also like freshwater fishing better than salt."

Davisson nodded. "I have to make a stop first. I manage a factory that makes animal food, mostly dog biscuits. I need to check something there."

"You're kind to a stranger," Cannert said, smiling. "A lot of folks down here in Florida have been. Sure makes me glad I came." He sighed. "Someone's still on my side, I guess."

Davisson nodded in the half darkness.

At the plant, Davisson opened the gate, drove through, then got out and relocked it.

"Company regulations," he explained.

He parked in front of the building. From the bed of the truck he got his package and then leaned in Cannert's window.

"Come in and take a look. It's mostly dials and switches and the like, but you might find the automation interesting. During the day I've got men who help, but I could do it all myself if I really had to."

Cannert obediently followed Davisson inside. Once they were in the office, Davisson's demeanor changed from accommodating to commanding.

"Sit there in that chair, old man. Tell me exactly where you're from and why you came to Centralia. And don't lie. I think I've seen you in my neighborhood."

Cannert gave him a surprised, frightened look. "I've already told you. I came down from Chicago. I don't remember ever seeing you before, sir."

"I've seen you," Davisson said, unconvinced. "Tell me or I'll make you sorry."

"I'm already sorry," Cannert said.

"You say you don't have any relatives or friends here?"

"No. None. Maybe there's a few folks I've met in bars or at the dog track." He gave Davisson an uneasy, concerned look. "If you want my money, I'll give it to you."

"I'll take it anyway, for the cause," Davisson said coolly. "No hurry. Do you know anything about animal foods?"

"No, sir."

"They're made from grains, mostly corn. Then there's bone meal, chicken, beef, pork. Our brand sells good because it has more meat and bone content than most. Out there in the plant there are machines that grind and mix, form, then cook and bake. I'm going to slip you into one of those machines, old man, and in about five hours you'll be in a sack. Your bones and your body will be ground down and cooked under pressure, mixed with thousands of pounds of other meat and grains. You'll be worth more then than now."

"You're joking," Cannert said softly.

"No. I don't joke." Davisson pointed. "I'll just drag you out to the first machine beyond that wall," he said, enjoying Cannert's discomfort. "There's a hoist I can use to haul you up and in. That machine cooks hot. I like to put you old ones inside it while you're still alive. I can watch what happens through a thick window in the front."

"I read something in the paper," Cannert said emptily. "I almost didn't come here because of it. You've done this before."

"Lots of times." Davisson smiled. "My company pays me bonuses for efficiency. I hate all you old ones."

Cannert sat quietly, feigning stunned disbelief.

Davisson continued, warming to his oratory. "I read the other day where people moving into Centralia had slowed way down. I guess I caused some of that. You should have gone elsewhere.

"Before I put you in the machine, I'm going to do some unpleasant things. They'll hurt a lot, but it'll be over soon enough, and I'll find out all there is to know about you. Then, when you're in the machine, I'll press these buttons here, one every time the light above it turns green. In less than five hours, you'll be part of our best and most expensive dog food."

He glanced over at the board, calculating. "Your bag numbers should start at about 6,150,200 and run on for five or six hundred bags. Tomorrow, they'll load you out to market."

"Those buttons there?" Cannert asked, as if not comprehending.

"Yes," Davisson answered, opening his package. Inside, there was a new rope, a long, iron rod, and an evil-looking whip. "I went prowling tonight and found you."

"My wife vanished down around here," Cannert said. "Large woman, gray hair, driving a '76 Plymouth with Illinois plates."

Davisson shrugged. "Too damn many of you. Too many. I hate you all. Too much blacktop, too many interstates, condos, apartments, motels. But I'll stop it."

"Do you remember her? Did you bring her here?"

"I don't know. I don't particularly remember her, but if I did, you'll soon join her." He smiled grimly. "It's going to start happening now." He picked up the iron rod. Cannert saw that it was cruelly barbed. "We'll start with this."

Cannert rose to his feet.

"Stay in that chair," Davisson ordered.

Cannert saw that the man wasn't, at the moment, completely sane. "Could I kneel and say a final prayer?"

Davisson considered the request. "You can pray only if

you pray to me, old man. There's no room for other deities here."

"To you, then," Cannert nodded. He slid off the chair onto his knees. For a moment, his body hid his hands. It was enough.

From a busy post office in Tampa, three weeks later, Cannert sent Davisson's driver's license to Lieutenant Ryan, c/o the Precinct Bar and Grill. He mailed it with two sacks—which were partly dogfood, partly Davisson.

Dog Man

"Can you still do it?" Ed Carter asked Dab. "I mean make friends with dogs you've never seen before? Control them?"

Dab nodded carefully. "Most times."

Ed nodded and remembered Nam. Dab had been able to control them then. The meanest dog, even a dog belonging to the angry little men in the black pajamas, frisked around him, tail wagging, waiting for a pat or a gentle word. He could talk turtles into popping their heads out of their shells. Birds, even large predatory ones, would come close to him and allow themselves to be fed. Ed had seen them, at times, land on his shoulder or hand. Dab had an instinctive feel for when to touch wild creatures and when not to. Sometimes, watching Dab with animals, Ed had felt as if he were another species, in one world, with Dab in another.

It wasn't a gift without problems. Their tent at base camp in Nam had been an area zoo. Officers learned not to closely inspect it. It was clean enough, but it was inhabited by snakes, lizards, tramp cats who'd escaped the native cooking pots, and mostly dogs. Dab was closest to dogs. Around George Dabney the animals lived in uneasy, watchful peace with each other, competing only for a place in Dab's sun.

His full name was George Andrew Dabney, Dab to Ed Carter. They sat now in a motel bar on the outskirts of Indianapolis. The bar seemed constructed half of plastics and half of indirect lights. A cute waitress, whose largest item of clothing seemed to be a bunny tail, industriously replenished drinks when they got low, smiling at them, working for a big tip.

"Why did you send for me?" Dab asked curiously. "I haven't heard from you since the service. I knew you were going back to law school and somebody said you'd finished and were working in Memphis. Then, all of a sudden, an airplane ticket."

"I need you to get inside a place. There are fifteen or twenty guard dogs on the grounds. I tried drugging hamburger meat, I tried a cattle prod, but there were too many of them. I want you to get me past them."

Dab shook his head primly. "I can't do that. It's illegal."

"And so?" Ed asked. "Getting out of that prison camp in Nam was legal? Stealing food out of native villages was legal?"

"We didn't hurt anyone. All I did was stop the dogs from barking. You were a part of my shadow. If I take you into a guarded place then I become a part of your aura or shadow, I'm responsible for you."

"What's this aura-and-shadow business?"

Dab shrugged. "A theory. Maybe just a guess. But I live by it."

"All you have to do is get me past some guard dogs," Ed said, acting exasperated.

"You don't understand, Ed. The way I believe it works is that animals with limited intelligence understand me and I also understand them, especially dogs. You want me to take you past guard dogs who've been trained to do something, to protect something or someone. I respect what they've been taught. I'll challenge it to save my life, but not for an illegal purpose."

"I need you bad, Dab," Ed said. "In a few weeks this

wife-beating psycho I'm after will take off into the islands and I'll be cooked."

"I'm sorry."

"I don't remember you being squeamish."

"I'm squeamish because the gift is still with me. I don't and won't make any animal do something it shouldn't do. They instinctively know that. So they trust me. If I violate that trust I know the ability to do what I do will be damaged. And the gift means something to me. It makes me unique. It's been my reason lately for living."

"I didn't know you were having problems."

Dab leaned forward. "I had a wife. She divorced me. I loved her, but she never saw or believed it, never felt anything. I'm not good with girls like you. I've had a host of jobs, but none of them have lasted. I'm not real smart and I know it. I don't know enough about animals to work with them full time even though I've tried to learn. I wanted to be a vet, but books are a puzzle. I can read, but what I read vanishes someplace. I only know how to make animals believe in me. I get called in on things now and then. I have a small reputation. And so I live, sometimes well, sometimes badly. You, you're smart. You make your living being smart."

"I'll let you make up your own mind," Ed said persuasively. "I'll tell you about what I'm going to do and then you can say yes or no."

"All right. I'll listen. But tell me only the strict truth. Don't add to it and don't subtract from it. It's important to both of us you do it that way. It could be dangerous any other way. This is no longer Nam."

"I represent a client," Carter said, nodding soothingly. "She married a man seven years ago. It was an unfortunate marriage in many ways. He was a very cruel man. It was fortunate in one. He made, they made, money. Over the years they quarreled, then fought, then wound up in divorce court. He took the jointly owned money and ran."

Dab smiled bitterly. "Except for the money it sounds like Shirley and me."

"She got a judgment against him for a part of the community property, but she's been unable to get any of it. He came to a place he owns a hundred-plus miles or so from Indianapolis, across the state line in Kentucky. Once, a few years back, they lived there together."

"You said there were dogs. Where do they come in?"

"He raised then and raises now guard dogs, Alsatians, German shepherds, some Dobies. Trains them. I know these things because I'm her lawyer. I know also that trying to get him into court again won't work in the time span I have available. In the northern Kentucky county where he now lives he has certain powers with the local officials, powers he's purchased. He's blood relation to the sheriff. I file something, his lawyers smile and delay, delay. So I have a valid judgment and no legitimate way to enforce it. If there was time I could do it legally, but there isn't time. He's about to run further, to a place I'll never be able to chase him. I'm now desperate. Time's run out. I remembered you. You're my last hope."

"And you say the money, or what you want of it, is her money?"

Ed nodded.

Dab nodded, taking Ed at his word. Ed smiled inwardly. His recollection of Dab was that he'd never been very acute, always been easy to lead, to convince, a dull, strange man, lost in his odd animal-dominated world. But they'd been friends once, or at least companions in an escape and in the long run from north to south. They'd survived.

"Can I see the judgment?" Dab asked cautiously.

"Sure." Ed had the bogus one he'd personally authored. It looked more genuine than a real one, with extra seals

and ribbons. He handed it across the table. Dab read it
slowly, his lips moving.

"And all I've got to do is get you past his dogs?"

"That's it. Once I'm inside and get her share I can go
from his house into his garage and take one of the cars.
You'll notice the judgment gives her a choice of vehicles.
He's got a remote-control device in every car to open the
gate. I get what's hers and then, in addition, take a car for
her. We drive away."

"What happens if he's there or has other people there?"

"There isn't anyone else. I won't have to hurt him. He's
a wife-beating coward, Dab. He won't fight."

"What's in it for me?"

"Two thousand."

Dab gave him a curious look. "What's in it for you?"

"A third of the recovery," Ed said. That was a lie, but it
was the fee he'd once been promised. Now it meant inde-
pendence and Marge. They'd use her husband's money to
finalize her divorce, to pay off his problems. Then they'd
use the rest of the money for the good life. If possession
was nine tenths of the law then they'd have possession and
Jack could come back into a state where there were a
hundred warrants out for him to contest that possession.
And, as Jack had done when he'd fled Marge and Tennes-
see, she, make that *they*, would take it all.

"No violence?" Dab asked. "You promise that? You have
to especially promise no guard dog is hurt."

Ed shook his head. "If he's there I may have to impress
him, frighten him, but I'm a lot bigger than he is and I
won't hurt him or any of the dogs." The gun in his belt felt
a little uncomfortable as he said it. If Jack Edgeworth was
there—and the chances were strong he would be, and
offered fight—then there could be violence. And if Dab
saw it and complained there could be double violence. Big
money. And Marge's hate for Jack Edgeworth was now Ed

Carter's hate. He'd heard her horror stories and believed them, at least for now.

"How soon do you need to know?" Dab asked.

"In the morning. I've booked us rooms here for the night. Think it over, read over the judgment, then tell me at breakfast. Eight in the morning?"

Dab nodded.

In the night Ed came awake and plotted against the day. Marge Edgeworth had come to him secondhand. Another lawyer had filed her divorce, then sat on it too long, and Jack, her husband, had fled Memphis for the northern Kentucky farm where he raised his dogs, the inherited place his family left him. He'd fired his man there and holed in. The money she claimed half of was hot money, money obtained by fraud. She'd come to Ed when his life was breaking down around him, making his decision easier. She knew about him some way, perhaps from her first lawyer. She knew he had disciplinary people from the state bar on his back and no way to pay the money back into the estate he'd pilfered from.

She knew, most of all, that time was running out for him. They needed each other.

She came into his office wearing a touch of both perfume and class. She had a big ring on her third left finger and her clothes were expensive. He didn't think she was beautiful, but the longer he watched her the more aware he became of her. She was tall and well formed. She moved like a tennis player, which he found she'd once been. She was, he estimated, five years older than he was, twenty years younger than mean Jack. Everything about her was physically right. Her eyes were lake-blue with the whites so clear and clean that they shone in the half light of the office. Her hair was white-blond and short. Physically perfect, stunningly constructed.

She outlined the problem in short words, as aware of him as he was of her. As Dab knew animals Ed Carter knew women. That's where the estate money had gone, fast women, beautiful horses. And he also knew, watching her, that this one was a woman for him.

The money came from a land con job. They'd done that together, but she swore her part had been only to be a come-on, to smile and serve the drinks, to act, but not be available. Her name was on nothing. No one was looking for her. The con was selling building lots on a lake project, big country club-style plans, but no money ever spent. There was a lot of money. It was in a safe, too heavy for one man to carry, a safe neighbors had told her that Jack and the soon-to-be-fired farm manager had carried into the farmhouse. She thought the combination would be the same. She'd been the one who set it, the instructions were still in her possession, and if he'd opened it he'd done it by force.

"Tell me about the money," Ed had said.

"Most of the lots sold from twenty thousand to fifty thousand, financed through banks, half the money up front. We carried mortgages on the other half, due in ten years. We sold more than three hundred lots in the first month alone. Thereafter it got slow. The money was supposed to go into an escrow fund for the lake, the roads, and the golf course, but it went into the safe instead." She shook her head. "He was doing all right before. He didn't need to get cute on the lake."

"But he did do it that way? And the money's still there?"

She nodded and shrugged, watching him. "He'd stay where he is now, but the tax people are now sniffing around. So he'll run." She said it with assurance.

He nodded and watched her. She smiled. Her eyes were Medusa-wise. By afternoon they were in a bar. By nightfall they were in bed.

He'd tried legal maneuvers first. He hired a lawyer for cocounsel in the county-seat town near where Jack lived. They got Jack into court only once, but Ed's cocounsel had seemingly lost interest. The hearing lasted half an hour and they lost. Ed talked to Marge about proceeding with her divorce in Memphis and chasing Jack from that home base. She coldly told him about a numbered account in Nassau and then mentioned a couple of quiet banana republics where Jack had friends. She talked about the tax people and what would happen if they got there first. She intended to stay married to Jack for whatever leverage that gave her—until she got the money.

Ed thought some more about the money. It was now her money, therefore his money.

He tried going alone over his farm fence. He was afraid to hire anyone. The money was too much to chance and he thought he could wind up buried deep. There were lots of dogs, big dogs. He wore heavy clothing, huge gloves, boots, and a plastic motorcycle helmet. Some of the dogs took the baited hamburger and died, but others, better trained, didn't. He burned his left leg with the cattle prod. It would keep one dog off, but not more than one. They came at him front, back, and sides. He felt lucky to get back over the fence alive. He considered trying to kill all the dogs with a rifle or dynamite but figured that Jack would then be waiting inside, alert and wary, armed and ready.

For a good chance he needed to get in soft and still. He needed to take Jack unawares.

For three long nights that first trip he waited outside the high fence with a rifle, but Jack stayed inside, perhaps sensing him out there. A sheriff's car then started patrolling the area and that drove Ed off. He thought Jack knew about Marge and him. Jack had sneered at him openly that one time in court. Maybe he had people watching Marge.

In the morning Dab agreed.

They drove into Blassport at about eight that night. It was still light and the house and its defending dogs were outside town on securely fenced acreage. They drove into a neoned drive-in and had hamburgers and fries and tall Cokes and fought the summer moths which came in the car windows. Ed stayed in the car on the off chance someone would see him, recognize him, and call Jack.

It got dark, no moon, light clouds.

The house sat behind the tall fence with a triplicate of barbed wire at the top. There was no light from Jack's windows, but that meant nothing. The night remained moonless. Dogs drifted along the fence as they drove past. Some of them barked. Ed kept on going and parked the rented car in a spot he'd used before, a quarter of a mile past the edge of Jack's land.

At the fence the night air smelled of summer leaves and animals. They went up and over.

In moments they were surrounded by a sea of big dogs. The dogs seemed not to know what to do. Some of them whined. Some of them came to Dab for a pat. Some of them trailed silently behind, watchful, waiting. There was no noise. Ed nodded at Dab, pleased.

"As advertised," he whispered. He counted more than a dozen dogs. He figured Jack opened the kennel gates at night and let all the dogs roam.

They went toward the house. The dogs crowded around Dab and it was eery to watch them with him. It was as if they were a pack and he was the leader of that pack. *Dog man.*

Marge had sketched a plan of the house which indicated the best door to enter and even provided a key she'd kept which she thought Jack had forgotten by now. Ed put it in the lock and turned it slowly while Dab stood outside, the dogs around him, some of them whining a little now.

Inside the house it was dark, but Ed could see light coming from one door, hear the sound of a radio or television. He walked back that way, the rug deadening all sound.

Jack sat in front of the TV. One old, grizzled dog lay near him. Ed went inside the room and put the barrel of the gun against Jack's ear, wanting the older man to do something so he could kill him.

"If that dog does anything or you do anything you're a dead man, Jack." He cocked the pistol so that Jack could hear the sound.

"Where's the safe?" he asked.

"In the bedroom."

"You and I are going there. If the dog wakes up you tell him to stay or I'll kill the dog and you." Ed nodded downward. "I came for Marge's share of the money."

"She'll never let you stay alive to spend it, lawyer boy. She's had a dozen like you, fancy young ones. They come to her like flies to honey. But she's not sweet, she's poison. I know her. She tried to have one of her bed pals kill me down there. When that didn't work and I ran she hired you. Did she tell you I beat her? Look at me. I weigh a hundred and thirty and had a heart attack three years back. She's twice as strong as me."

"I don't believe a word you're saying," Ed said. "We're going to get married."

"You're no more to her than the rest."

"Let's go to the safe," Ed said more loudly. The dog heard him and came awake. He growled once, old but still formidable. Jack patted him.

"Stay," he said.

The dog whined.

They went out the door and found another room down the hall. Jack turned on the light.

"You work the combination," Ed said.

"Sure. Read it to me. She had charge of the money. She figured out and ran the land game. I never had the combination. I've been living on what was here in the bank. Next week a man was coming to drill the safe."

Ed read him the combination. He watched Jack's sweaty hands work the combination, turn the handle, and open the safe.

Then it went wrong. Maybe the gun was in the safe, maybe somewhere else, but suddenly Jack had a gun.

Ed shot him twice. From the television room he heard the old inside dog bark loudly.

Jack sprawled on the floor. Ed kicked the gun away from him and watched Jack's eyes film over. He perceived movement at the door to the room and turned. Dab was there watching. When Ed turned he left the doorway and vanished.

Ed took a pillowcase and put money in it from the safe. There was too much for one pillowcase so he got another.

The inside dog was snarling and scratching at the door to the room where he'd been left, making more noise than Ed wanted. He fired one shot through the door and all sound stopped.

He got to the first car all right. It was a fairly new Cadillac. The garage door was down so he found and pushed a control on the visor and saw the door rise. Dab stood outside in the drive with the dogs. He was watching Ed.

"You said no trouble," he said loudly. "The dogs remember you. You killed some of them before. You killed their man tonight."

"Jack had a gun."

"These dogs may kill me now," Dab said, his voice dropping.

"They will. I shot a dog inside, too. Get in the car. I owe you two thousand dollars. I'll pay you at the gate. I'll take you where you want to go."

"No. I can't do that. I have to stay."

"Come on, Dab. They're only dogs."

"No." Dab's eyes were strange. Ed thought he saw tears in them.

Ed shrugged and turned on the key and pushed the button for the power window by the driver. "I can't just leave you here," he said logically. "There's the sheriff. You'd tell all you know." He fired once at Dab and wasn't sure whether he'd hit him. The pack of dogs surged angrily around the car. One tried to come up through the window, but Ed had it rolling up by that time and the big shepherd bounced off, starring the window a bit.

Dab put his head and one arm around the edge of the garage door. He held up something in his hand. Ed went cold when he saw what it was. Three somethings. Three distributor caps. One for each car in the garage.

"You're on your own," he said. He turned away.

Ed turned the key to turn the motor on. The starter whirred, but the motor wouldn't start.

"Help me, Dab," he called desperately. "Half the money."

"Come out of the car and tell me about it," Dab said. He nodded at the dogs. "My deal was with them. You violated it. You lied." He nodded. "You'll have to come out of the car soon. I've let them know that. They're willing to wait. They're withholding decision on me until that time. When you come out maybe I can go, but it'll never be the same for me again. You did that, Ed."

Ed fired another shot at him through the windshield, but all it did was make a hole and weaken the safety glass. Dab vanished around the corner. Ed could hear him whistling to the animals there, crooning to them, maybe petting one or two that came close, making allies.

Ed found he was already thirsty.

Some of the dog pack growled and waited by the doors to the car. One jumped on the hood and scratched at the windshield, but it held.

For the moment.

Whistler

"I'd like you to go with me to Hill Hospital today," Senator Adams said. He nodded me toward the old leather couch in his office. He then made an alleyway between the law-books stacked on his desk so he could see me. I sat. He was obviously researching something and I was pretty sure I knew what it was. The stacks of books piled on his desk, in corners, and here and there on the floor were even larger than usual.

"What are you researching?" I asked, to confirm my suspicions.

"Insanity," he said. "It seems to be a poor defense. We let lay jurors determine sanity in the same trial they're also primarily asked to determine guilt or innocence."

"You don't agree with our laws on sanity?" I asked, unshocked.

He gave me a somewhat sour look. "Read the case reports, Robak. They'll show you that few people using the defense do well if the crime charged was violent."

"Hill Hospital and Sam Whitley are what you're thinking on then?"

He nodded.

Hill was a mental hospital.

"What time do you go?"

"About three this afternoon. I'd like you with me when I talk with Dr. Ansberg and perhaps see Sam Whitley."

"I've an appointment for then," I said. "And Sam Whitley's your client, not mine."

"Please change your appointment." He gave me an apologetic look. "For me it's doctor's orders. You inherit the case."

"Thank you," I said. Some small sarcasm may have shown through for he gave me a sharp look. I kept my own face impassive by busying myself looking around his cluttered office. Sam Whitley had been indicted on two counts of murder and, from what I'd read in the local paper, the prosecutor had no proof problems. Area media had viciously reported all the bloody facts of the murders.

I was three years into the practice of law at that time. I was still sure of many things. I got better at being unsure as I grew older and watched the world undo itself around me.

"Sam cut my yard when he was a boy," the senator said in explanation.

He was no longer a state senator, but the name had stuck. Once a state senator always a state senator.

"I heard your yard cutter exploded again at the jail and it got to be a toss-up whether Judge Steinmetz would send him to the reformatory to await trial or on to Hill Hospital for observation," I said.

"He did go berserk again. He isn't large, but it took three deputies to overpower him. Judge Steinmetz held a hearing and sensibly decided he needed to be examined at Hill." He smiled and looked out his grimy window at the city of Bington below, now in full-leaf summer. The city was his love now that his wife was gone. He was a good man, but sometimes his ideas on the law and how it should operate were odd. He gave me a penetrating look. "Tell me your opinion on the current state of the insanity defense."

"In Sam Whitley's case?"

"Yes."

"It won't mean a thing. The prosecutor will undoubt-

edly present a dozen witnesses to testify Whitley was sane
and normal around the time of the murders. Even if we
get favorable opinions from psychiatrists it's up to a jury to
make the final decision and you know few violent murderers get off. Of course if psychiatrists testify and then Judge
Steinmetz rules Whitley not sane enough to assist us or
stand trial then we'd be off the hook until that changed."

He nodded again.

"What made you take the case?" I asked bluntly. "I
mean here's a man who, in a fit of rage, lays in wait and
kills his estranged wife and her lover with an ax. The
newspapers keep calling him Sam Borden. I suppose that's
after Lizzie Borden of forty-whacks fame. It isn't your
kind of case."

"I remembered him as a boy. Also Judge Steinmetz appointed me—us—to defend him." He shook his head
sadly. "When Sam cut my yard and Steinmetz's yard down
the street he whistled and smiled all the time he was
working. A happy boy then. A whistler."

"So we go to Hill Hospital this afternoon to see if the
psychiatrists will say your whistler's sane enough for
trial?"

"Yes. I called Dr. Ansberg last night. He's an old friend.
He told me Sam's coming along slowly. I'd like you to read
the file and be ready to go with me today."

I took the file and hefted it. "Thin," I said. "Very light."

"There's a few things you won't find in there. The new
boy friend had moved in with Sam's wife. He was a volunteer part-time deputy sheriff. He ran Sam off with a gun
twice when Sam went there attempting a reconciliation.
Sam lost one family to a fire and a cheating wife to a man
with a gun." He looked at me and shook his head. "She
laughed at Sam."

I called and changed my appointment. It didn't make me like Sam Whitley's case any better. It was a dead sure loser.

The file contained both Whitley's juvenile record and his adult record, a copy of an old presentence report, plus a sheaf of news stories about the murders and Sam's arrest. There were also two scathing editorials clipped from the pages of the local paper. That paper has, down the years, found it profitable to be against major and minor sins.

Whitley had come whistling out of what seemed to be a normal boyhood. He'd been in no trouble until after he was fifteen. His intelligence was slightly below normal, but not low enough to take him out of regular school. In his fifteenth year he'd been orphaned in a home fire in which his parents, older sister, and younger brother had died. He'd been the sole scorched survivor. A Christmas tree fire, lights left on after the family had gone to bed.

Maybe we could lean on that, stir up sympathy. It might keep him off death row.

Maybe.

His problems had begun after the fire. There'd been social security and so he'd been a wanted commodity. Custody had originally passed to an aged uncle who'd used the money Sam had brought for his alcohol habit. That arrangement hadn't lasted. There'd been a string of foster homes. There'd soon been drugs and break-ins, stolen cars, and fights. He'd robbed a grocery store with a cap pistol and drawn a term at Youth School. He'd critically knifed another inmate there, a bigger, older boy who'd threatened him sexually. Then, when Sam had turned eighteen and become eligible for adult prison, he'd soon made it.

I looked over the record. From the bare bones I could see nothing he'd done had ever been clever or planned well. *A dumbhead.*

On parole he'd married and for a time had stayed out of

trouble. She'd cheated and he'd caught her, beaten her savagely, and so gone back to prison. She'd filed for divorce. When his sentence was up Sam had followed her to her family home out Moss Road near the river. Police theorized in news articles that if her mother had been home she might also have died by the avenging ax. Sam had hewed wife and boy friend to bits, then charged the police who'd come at a neighbor's call, still swinging the bloody ax. What was left of Sam's wife and her lover had been found scattered about the house.

I thought about the pictures that would be introduced at trial and shook my head.

No chance for the whistling boy. Life or death.

Dr. Ansberg was a tall, old man with a fringe of dyed black hair around an otherwise bald head. He had a hard-to-believe Viennese accent and his face consisted mostly of bright dentures. He clasped the senator's hand warmly and I could see they liked each other. He nodded formally at me when we were introduced.

"Your partner and I have known each other for many years. When I first came to this country I met him at church. He helped me greatly, Mr. Robak."

"You helped me also, Doctor," the senator said. "You talked me back to work when my wife died. You went out of your way." He smiled at Ansberg and at me. I'd found he had a thousand friends and that he deserved them. Sometimes I didn't understand him, but I loved the old man.

"The senator saved me," Ansberg continued.

"How's that?" I asked, interested.

"When I came here they were going to fire me from this place. That was when my English wasn't so good. I was already growing old and my wife was ill. There were many reasons I needed my job here." He smiled and the dentures sparkled. "The senator made one phone call and my job was saved. He charged me nothing. He wouldn't even send me a bill."

The senator looked embarrassed. "Enough. Tell us about our man Whitley."

"He grows better," Dr. Ansberg said, smiling tranquilly. "Perhaps soon we'll have him able to assist you in his trial."

"But you and those helping you couldn't testify he's sane and competent now?"

"I believe not yet. When they assigned him to me he was still quite violent. Paranoid schizophrenia. We tranquilized him. There are truly remarkable drugs available for many purposes these days. He fell into a pattern which I could predict. He first forgot what had happened. The drugs allowed him to withdraw from life for a time. He's now turned back a bit toward us and life. He remembers his childhood, his early youth, his happy times. He has no memory yet of the fire which took his family, his prison days, or the killings. Those things are below the surface. They'll be the last to return. I believe he has vague dreams of them, flashes, insights into himself. With the drugs all seems well most of the time." He nodded. "We push him along the stream. My prognosis is he'll soon be well enough to stand trial." He looked out the window of his office and got up. "Come see him yourselves."

I followed the senator to the window. Outside white-clad attendants and patients moved slowly or briskly, as they desired, under the warm summer sun. Some patients gazed vacantly, others seemed occupied with themselves.

"Sun time," Dr. Ansberg said. "This time of year we try to get even those who've lost all contact with us out into the summer world."

I recognized Sam Whitley from newspaper pictures. He was accompanied by two attendants, both of them burly men. Sam came smiling down the walk, his stride boyish. He was, I knew, in his early thirties.

The senator shook his head sadly. "Too bad for him he can't remain the way he now is and come no further."

Dr. Ansberg regarded the senator solemnly. "Yes? Too bad?"

"Soon he'll be trying to swim in rough seas, trying to live or die," the senator said. "The prosecutor talked to me earlier today." He looked over at me and frowned. "He's going for the death penalty." He looked away from me and back down at Sam Whitley, who walked lightly and uncaringly on.

"That's unfair," I said. "It was a family thing. Certainly his wife had given him provocation. There's the unwritten law." I thought quickly about the trial to come, about bloody clothes, gory color pictures, and a semicompetent prosecutor running for his political life in an election year. "It's unfair," I said again.

"Life's unfair," the senator said evenly. He nodded at the happy boy-man below. "Unfair, but legal."

Dr. Ansberg watched only Senator Adams. His eyes were serious as he watched; his smile had vanished.

Ansberg and another doctor from Hill Hospital appeared in court ten days later and testified Sam Whitley was still unable to assist his attorneys in his defense. Judge Steinmetz continued the matter.

Prosecutor Paul Roberts, sensing trial delay past election time, held an angry press conference, then filed a new petition asking that other psychiatrists be appointed to examine Sam Whitley. Steinmetz denied it without a hearing. The prosecutor made vague statements about an appeal, but none was filed. He did use what had happened in his campaign speeches. Judges are easy for the public to hate even when they're right.

Summer dragged into fall. In November Roberts narrowly lost his bid for another term as prosecutor. Senator Adams and I bought each other a celebration drink.

After the election a rapist-murderer terrified the local university campus. He killed three young women in Jack the Ripper style. The news media forgot Sam Whitley and took up a new cause. Then a many times convicted drunk driver, operating without a license, drove a plush stolen auto unerringly into six schoolchildren waiting for a school bus. All of the children were under ten. The driver killed two, maimed two more. Angry protesters paraded in front of the jail and courthouse.

Sam Whitley grew cooler.

The new prosecutor came and conferred calmly with Senator Adams and me about Whitley and his circumstances.

"They say he's still about as he was," he said. "I went up there to Hill and his doctor, a nice old man named Ansberg, was very cooperative. He let me see him in his ward. I wasn't allowed to ask questions. Ansberg explained that Whitley's hold on reality is quite fragile."

Senator Adams nodded. "If you'd have asked one of us would have gone along. Within the limits of what Dr. Ansberg would have allowed we'd have let you ask him whatever you wanted."

Alvin Koontz, the new prosecutor, said, "I really don't need anything from him. We've a God's plenty of evidence sitting in the police lock room gathering dust. All I need is for the hospital people to say he's competent to stand trial."

"We're ready when Whitley's ready," the senator said. "You were the one most recently at Hill. What did Ansberg tell you?"

Koontz smiled. He was a good man and an excellent lawyer. The senator and I both approved of him.

"He said Sam Whitley was still hiding back in his boy-hood. Dr. Ansberg took me past the locked ward where they keep him. He was whistling and bouncing a ball off a wall and trying to catch it." He shook his head. "He had a big smile. He seemed happy. Yes, happy." He looked out the senator's window at the snow falling on Bington's dirty downtown. "It was a better day than today. I tried to talk with the other doctor, but he didn't have much to say. Ansberg appears to be very much the one in charge. He seemed to think Sam Whitley might stay as he is for a long time, still living a fantasy life around the age of fourteen or so, unmarred by all that happened afterward." Koontz seemed uneasy about it. "Is that possible, Senator?"

"I suppose. What are your intentions, Alvin?"

"I'll prosecute him if he recovers, gentlemen. I looked over the file. I don't know for certain that I'd ask for the death penalty."

"You're generous in thinking of that."

Koontz shook his head. "Not generous. It's only that time has passed. And Ansberg seems to think that Sam Whitley may stay in limbo. He could go either way tomorrow or stay as he is. If he doesn't recover I suppose we'll never prosecute him. You gentlemen know the law doesn't allow that." He smiled once more. "The thing that really got to me in seeing him was that he seemed happy."

"He's had much unhappiness. You know his history?"

"I've looked at his file, Senator. I know about the fire and his dead wife's reputation."

"Perhaps he's already had his punishment," the senator said, his eyes strange. He seemed nervous, slightly upset. "Maybe it works that way. Some of us get our punishment up front and commit our crimes afterward."

"The Campus Creeper didn't. We start trial on him next month. He's nineteen and comes from a good family, Senator." He shook his head in disbelief. "Nineteen . . ." He thought for a moment. "Then there's that multiple-vehicle homicide case to try. No rest for an already weary new prosecutor."

Perhaps things would have stayed *in status quo* longer, but Ansberg suffered a heart attack in May.

I heard about it when I arrived at the office on a bright morning. The senator was already there, moving about his office restlessly, shelving books, discarding papers, and obviously waiting for me.

"Dr. Ansberg's over in the Bington Hospital in intensive care. He's sent word he wants to see me. You can come if you say nothing—no matter what Ansberg says—while we're with him. I want you to come. Ansberg's wife is long dead, his only daughter was last heard of in a commune and can't be found and he had no sons."

"Why does he want to see you?"

He shrugged. He seemed calm.

"Did you know Ansberg had medical problems?"

"We're both of that age," he said, smiling now. "Terminal."

I tagged along because he wanted me. I drove him to the hospital.

Intensive care was on the fifth floor. A stout nurse led us down a quiet hall and gave us stern instructions. She shook her head when the senator inquired concerning Ansberg's condition.

Ansberg lay quietly in a hospital bed. He seemed shrunken. He had tubes in one nostril. A suspended bottle dripped clear fluid into another tube needled into his arm. He had wires attached to his arms and chest. Someone had removed the too-white dentures.

The room smelled of antiseptic and ammonia.

Ansberg's eyes were still alert but wounded. They followed Senator Adams across the hospital room.

"Sit," Ansberg ordered him in a hoarse whisper, ignoring me.

The senator pulled up a metal folding chair. I found an inconspicuous place near the window of the small room.

Ansberg began without preamble. Each word seemed an effort. "I think your man Sam Whitley will now be all right."

"You mean he'll be competent to stand trial?" the senator asked.

"No, not that. I believe he'll remain always as he is now." He grimaced an imitation smile. "There are other disciplines than yours of law, Senator," he said carefully. "Surely you realize that?"

The senator shrugged.

Ansberg continued, "Sometimes, when I began to treat him, he seemed to be coming along despite what I did. I gave him shock treatments for a time until that stopped. I gave him other drugs than the tranquilizers. I spent hours —no, days—going over his early life with him, again and again. Progress stagnated. He believes now that he's contagiously ill and fancies someday he'll be well enough to be reunited with his family. His mind is no longer inquiring or curious. He wanted to forget. I helped him forget. He believes he's fourteen. Time has stopped for him, fourteen forever." Ansberg shook his head. "I've not had to do anything with him for a long while. Only the normal tranquilizers now."

Senator Adams leaned close to Ansberg, but I saw that the senator's eyes were on me. "I didn't ask you to do this, Doctor."

Ansberg's voice weakened. "I know. Perhaps I saw it wrong, read it poorly. What I've done might even be criminal. I know little of your laws. But there are more types of insanity than my profession yet has names for. If Sam Whitley recovers he must then stand trial, perhaps even die. You saw in Sam the boy who once was happy and made me see that boy also. Now he'll always be that boy. As once you gave me a free gift which meant my life I've now given a life gift to Sam Whitley in your name. I'll let your legal mind fumble about and decide whether what I've done is tolerable or not, whether it's 'right.' It may not be to you. Perhaps what I sensed in watching you was wrong. But believe *it is* the way I've revealed and can't be easily changed. You may, if you wish, ask that new psychiatrists be assigned for Sam Whitley at Hill. You may then tell them what I've done and what I'm telling you now. They'll find nothing in the medical charts to help them because I put very little there. Perhaps, but only perhaps, they'll manage to turn your Sam Whitley forward again if that's what you desire." He gave us the smile-grimace again. "If you do nothing then perhaps things will proceed at their normal, legal snail's pace. Sam Whitley will remain as he is and be soon forgotten. He'll stay always as he is now. Your choice, Senator." Once more he smiled his ghastly, joking smile, sans teeth.

The senator shook his head and looked inquiringly over at me. I realized, at that moment, that he'd at least suspected and probably known what was going on. Several times, in the past months, he'd visited Hill Hospital alone.

"That would let a guilty man escape punishment," he said.

"Yes," Ansberg admitted. "And something more. It might also let an insane man regain sanity, limited sanity, but a sanity which brought him happiness."

In the car I looked the senator over. "You're a most devious man. I'm sure you knew what Ansberg was doing."

He shook his head wearily. "I never knew for certain.

Perhaps I suspected." He faced me. "Don't start the motor yet. We need to make a decision."

"We need to get to Judge Steinmetz and tell him exactly what's happened," I said harshly.

"Think some on it. If Sam Whitley had been convicted what would have happened to him?"

"Perhaps the death penalty. Some get it."

"Come off it, Robak. You're a better lawyer than that. Koontz would have never tried to get it. Even if he had, at trial level or appellate level, after ten thousand hours of agonizing briefs and arguments, the death penalty would have vanished in smoke and we'd have won a great victory. What then would have happened to Sam Whitley?"

"A long time in prison."

"Yes, but eventually parole?"

"Maybe," I admitted grudgingly. "Usually."

"Almost assuredly if Sam lived long enough. Do you think that prison time would have turned Sam into a solid citizen?"

"I don't know." I thought about it and finally shook my head. "I suppose not."

"You know not. Isn't what's happening to him now, under Ansberg's cure, an effective method of containing Whitley?"

"It isn't a legal method."

"Quit being scandalized because the lawbooks don't specify it. You know they aren't the answer to all."

"People get out of mental hospitals also," I warned.

"No. Civilly committed people get out. Whitley can't get out. If he should move forward and become able, in the future, to assist in his defense then he goes back to jail and from there to trial. The evidence in this one will last until the last survivor witness dies. Think about it, Robak."

I thought. I thought for a long time.

Ansberg died four days later. Senator Adams died in 1974.

A few days ago I had the necessity, as judge, to go to Hill Hospital. There, after holding hearings, I paid a courtesy call on the new superintendent. He seemed harried and complained of being overworked and understaffed. I didn't mention Sam Whitley's name.

When I left his office I drove to the north gate, taking the route past the locked ward where Sam Whitley had once been held.

He was, I knew, no longer there.

Near the north gate, in front of a pleasant building surrounded by shrubs and flowers, I saw Sam Whitley. There were no longer guards watching him. I slowed and he gave my car a glance. He was now a little bent with age, not as spry as once he'd been, fiftyish. There was a basketball goal and he had a ball. He was pretty good. I waved and he nodded back to me, smiling. He then went intently back to his game.

I was almost sure he was whistling.

Savant

Dr. Morgan sat with his back to the office window and listened.

"The sheriff's out here again today," Mrs. Lord, the hospital administrator, said severely.

"I saw him around my building."

"They did the autopsy. He's seen the preliminary findings and he's not satisfied with them." Mrs. Lord looked out her window imperiously. "I'm not, either. A child just doesn't die without reason, even a child as profoundly retarded as Sandra."

"I'm puzzled about it also, but I'm afraid I can't add anything," Morgan said. He looked at his watch. It was time to be back on the ward that was the focal point of his life these days.

She looked critically down at a file that he presumed to be his and then over his head and out her window, surveying her domain. He knew she liked everything tidy, and he had no objection to its being that way as long as her orderliness didn't interfere in his life.

"Outside" was a state mental hospital, a gathering of ramshackle buildings, recreation areas, and farmland. Once it had been all retarded children, but a falling state budget had combined the children with adults. Tax money for the retarded and the mentally ill existed at the far edges of a politician's dream.

"Your appointment as a permanent staff member comes

up next month. What am I supposed to tell the board then?"

He shook his head cynically, not knowing, not particularly caring. A fourteen-year-old girl with a life history of profound mental retardation following postnatal cerebral infection had died. Most like that in his ward were forgotten, abandoned by their parents, unvisited and unwanted. But Sandra was one of the rare ones whose family still visited frequently, a family living close by the hospital. They'd gone to the prosecutor and sheriff. Investigators now prowled the halls of his wards, where the most profoundly retarded were, asking the attendants questions, making notes. The newspapers had gotten into the death recently. Their stories had been vague but suspicious.

"Nothing else unusual on your ward?" she asked carefully. Her degrees were in business, not medicine, and he and Mrs. Lord shared no common purpose. She was an administrator, he was a doctor.

"There's never anything usual on it. Children change. Even children who are profoundly retarded learn small, new things, develop new symptoms." He almost reminded her about Kelly but decided not to. Kelly was the one person on the ward whom investigators could talk to if Kelly wanted to talk. But Kelly was delicate and had her own problems. She was blind, retaining only the ability to tell light from shadow, and her days and strength were spent in eagerly sculpting the heads she remembered from when she'd had sight, or new ones she felt with her inquiring fingers.

A savant. Idiot savant. The sculpted heads were beautifully done, and Morgan had written to Kelly's family about them more than a year back—with no reply and now none expected. Kelly was twenty-six years old. Until a few years back, she'd been able to see but had not interacted well with her peers or the staff, nor had the gift. Morgan had read the reports. Loss of vision from glaucoma had sent her on a strange inward journey. When Morgan had come to the hospital, Kelly had not communicated. Now she talked, but only when she wanted to talk. The heads were her obsession.

Mrs. Lord went on for more minutes. Morgan, listening to her, found that he cared nothing about whether or not he was reappointed. There were other hospitals, and hospitals like this were so understaffed with doctors trained also as psychiatrists that even scandal wasn't likely to keep him from finding a new job. He was used to scandal. He knew he had drinking and drug problems. Mrs. Lord knew it also and had known it when he was hired. He thought she was examining him covertly today to see what shape he was in.

Not too bad, lady. I'm trying to cut back. Maybe one day I'll quit.

He escaped to the wards. Once there he took a strong pill to catch up. For a while he read the paper, but the news was, as usual, bad. Someone had assassinated another leader in India. Terrorists had commandeered a jetliner in Italy. The Soviets claimed they had new weapons, and new defenses against old weapons. The national debt was growing alarmingly.

Somehow the whole system had gone wrong and was so ponderous that no one could now change it. He put the paper into the wastebasket. The hate that still smoldered within him was reserved mostly for the system and those who kept it painfully going, fighting about money for weapons and money for hunger, wasting two units for every unit spent usefully, internationally preying savagely on each other. One day soon they'd have to use all those weapons, if only for the sake of economy, and blow the planet up.

The thought was not unsatisfying.

His wards were painted in calm colors. Children and adults lay in ugly wooden orthopedic carts, many of them home-crafted in the shops of the state hospital. The patients stared up at the ceiling, most of them seeing nothing, nonverbal and nonambulatory. Sandra had been like that. And then, without symptom or warning, she'd died.

He read the charts and visited the two wards he had primary responsibility for. He prescribed Dilantin, phenobarbital, Mellaril, Thorazine, and Valium for spasticity and seizures. He prescribed for constipation, incipient bedsores, and aggressive behavior. When he was exhausted and done, he illegally prescribed some Dilaudid for himself.

With that accomplished, he escaped to Kelly.

Kelly lay in her own cart. She was a thin, small woman with already graying hair. Her face was remote and unpretty. Morgan thought she was aware of what went on around her, that she heard everything. How much she understood of what she heard was questionable. He'd tried to give her the various intelligence tests available, but she'd been uninterested. He assessed her as brilliant in the area of her savantpower, dull to normal in all others.

Today Kelly was talkative.

"Man came in. Asked about girl who died. Wanted to know what I knew." She shook her head, upset somehow by the questioning.

Morgan waited. When Kelly stopped, Morgan prompted her, "What do you know, Kelly? What did you tell the man?"

"Made her head once. Her mother came and saw what I do. Brought Sandra close, and I touched and then made a face out of the clay." She looked up at the bright window that lay above her. "Can see her like she was. She was sick."

"How sick?" Morgan asked, interested.

Kelly answered as she usually did when her interest waned. "I don't know. You want me to make your head now?"

"Sometime. Soon now." He liked this child-woman, but the thought of her fingers on his face was repugnant to him. He no longer wanted to be close to any person.

At times he daydreamed that he was terminally ill and heavily armed, ready to take his own revenge on an uncaring world. It was something that could take his mind away from worse memories.

"I make heads, and Nurse Datal bakes so they last," Kelly said, happy about it.

"I know," Morgan said. "Why do you make the heads, Kelly?" He was feeling pretty good now, floating a little, all pain and remembrance dim. The wife and daughter who'd vanished in the flames no longer insistently called to him. He could forget them.

"See them inside my head." Kelly nodded, still happy. "Have to make them. Once I could see many things, but now what I see is inside my head."

Conversation waned. Morgan liked Kelly and sensed Kelly also liked him. It was enough to sit close to the cart, to be there, to make Kelly a tiny part of the thing he'd lost, an ersatz substitute.

For a time Morgan slept in the chair by Kelly's cart. He was awakened by a hand on his shoulder.

"I need to talk with you again, Dr. Morgan," Sheriff Boonburger ordered heavily. "So wake up."

Morgan nodded and got up. He led the sheriff to his office. He found in the walk there that he was trembly, and his watch told him it was past time for something, maybe some Demerol. His taste in drugs had become more catholic down the years.

Morgan took a chair, and the sheriff towered above him —squeaking leather belt, boots, and gun—making Morgan nervous, making him want to reach out and grab the gun and fire it until it was empty.

"I'm wondering if you got any new ideas on why the girl died?"

Morgan shook his head.

"You have charge of the ward. You give the pills out, prescribe for the patients here. The results of the drug tests on Sandra haven't come back yet, but the thought now is that she may have died from an overdose of something. What were you giving her?"

Morgan tried to remember. Except for Kelly, somehow the ward residents all seemed to fall into one mass of gasping, cruel mouths, sick and angry screams, dumb silence, and violent seizures. He reached for Sandra's chart. "She got Valium for spasticity and phenobarbital for seizures. She got some suppositories to ease elimination." He smiled without humor. "At the time she died, her worst medical situation appeared to be that she had hemorrhoids."

"How often did she have seizures?"

Morgan shrugged. "Sometimes she'd get two in one day. Sometimes, when we had her well controlled, she'd not get one for a month or two. She'd been in good shape for a month."

"Did she have some kind of seizure when she died?"

"You know she didn't, Sheriff."

The sheriff looked at him. "You don't volunteer a lot of information, do you, Doctor?"

"What do you want the information for?"

"To find out what happened."

"People have died here before. I'm sure you know that. These people lie for years in orthopedic carts, they're fed diet foods, they get no exercise except what the physical therapists give them. Most of them can't even tell us when something goes wrong. They tend to have strokes, heart problems. They seem to develop cancer more easily and more often than normal people." Morgan shook his head. "You weren't interested in the other deaths we've had here. Why the interest in this one?"

"Their fathers weren't on my county council," the sheriff said. "He don't like what happened, and therefore I don't like it, either. And when I checked on you, I didn't like what I got told, Doctor."

Morgan waited, feeling a chill run through him.

"One place we called said you were a practicing lush and a doper, that you'd had some accident tragedy in your family and it turned you into something with a bad smell to it. Some other places you've been were very evasive. I'm now wondering, if we don't find a cause for Sandra's death, if her old man would let us all off the hook and give up his crusade if you just packed on out of here—resigned?"

"Is that what you want?" Morgan asked. "Would that satisfy you and your local politicians?"

"Maybe, but not until all the results are in from the lab tests. Then we'll see what will satisfy my people."

Morgan found he was having trouble concentrating. He felt hot inside and he hurt all over. He needed something soon—codeine, Percodan, Darvon, Demerol. Something.

The sheriff moved to the door. "You wait," he warned. "Don't try to leave."

When the sound of footsteps had receded completely away, Morgan took another pill. He got a bottle out of the bottom drawer of his desk and had a long pull of vodka to wash the narcotic down.

Waking was the hardest thing. In sleep there was refuge because there were seldom dreams. But when he awoke, all the dreams that had gathered on the horizon and been unable to get through the wall of drugs and alcohol he had erected awaited him again. Awakening in the office was always to the odors of the hospital. The stench was a mixture of rot, urine, and coffee this morning.

He lay on the couch in his office. He remembered the accident, being thrown clear. He'd tried to walk, then finally to crawl to the burning car, but he'd been unable. All he could do was listen to the screams that came from the flames. Wife and six-year-old daughter. Beautiful daughter. Not like Kelly. Not ugly and blind.

The other driver had been drunk, had been driving his old uninsured clunker at high speed on the wrong side of the road with a suspended license. Nothing much had happened to him. A slap on the wrist. Six months, suspended.

Morgan had been sober and drug-free. But not afterward.

Others said it would only take time and he'd forget, but he'd not forgotten, and now it was five years.

Physician, heal thyself. He'd tried, but found no cure. And now he was as he was, competent enough when he wasn't too strung out on drugs or alcohol, but unable to hold a job for very long because of his almost visible habits. A year or two one place, six months at another. A hobo doctor, embittered, puzzling to his peers, and perpetually angry.

He got up and found black coffee. He examined his face in the mirror of his office. He noted without interest that he was thinner than he'd been, and wondered when he'd last eaten a real meal. He saw that his eyes seemed almost transparent. He took a pill. A pill or a drink was his cure for everything. He could rail at himself because it was that way, but he could no longer change it. He'd even turned himself in once, been on an addiction ward for sixty days, then gone immediately back to the drugs when released. After a binge.

He was, he decided, like the world around him, gravely ill, terminal. No hope.

He went out into the wards and managed the morning routine. Nothing untoward seemed to have happened. Those who wet the bed had wet the bed. Those who could feed themselves were now doing it with varying degrees of success. Attendants fed the others. Many of the patients were on special diets. The attendants he passed eyed him curiously, and he wondered what the stories about him were now. His interest in them was minor, but curiosity remained.

He knew that once, a long time back, five years now, he'd been a good doctor. He knew that now he no longer was. He hadn't read anything in those five years, and his interest in psychiatry and medicine continued only because it gave him access to the drugs he needed to survive a while longer. His only fascination was in his own bitterness and feeding it, in dreaming of the world's damnation.

At two the sheriff came. He motioned Morgan to his office. Morgan followed the bigger man. Sheriff Boonburger took his chair, so Morgan sat meekly in the other one.

"They've called a grand jury, Doc." The sheriff watched him curiously, perhaps seeking some reaction. Morgan felt pretty good, about right. He smiled and nodded.

"I think probably they'll indict you for involuntary manslaughter real quick," the sheriff said, relishing his bombshell, still watching.

"Why would they do that?"

"Maybe because this year's election year. The girl died. She was in your care. You got drug problems. So you'll get indicted. Sometime tonight or tomorrow. I'll come out for you then. They're going to ask for a big bond. That means you'll be boarding with me." He watched Morgan with snow-cold eyes. "When I put you in, I'm going to strip-search you. You won't have any pills to help you, no bottle of booze to hide behind. I figure you'll break wide open in maybe two or three days. You'll tell me anything I want to hear just because I want to hear it."

"But you know I wasn't even close to that girl when she died, and you have no evidence that I either failed to do something for her or did something to her that caused her death?"

"She's dead, Doc. She was your patient. I can smell your breath from here. I can read your eyes. I've seen guys like you a hundred times. I'm not fooled. You'll break for me."

"I see," Morgan said, not seeing, but realizing the finality of it.

He planned. He figured out what was available and what it would require. Enough of these and he'd go to sleep and not wake up, enough of those and he'd float off and drown in his own juices.

No one to say goodbye to. Maybe Kelly. He chose the drowners.

He took a massive dose and wandered out into the ward. By the time he got to Kelly, it was hard to see, hard to navigate. Death was a soon-to-be thing.

He took Kelly's hand and woke her up from sleep.

"I came to say goodbye," he said. He noticed clinically that his voice wasn't slurred yet, but that the rest of him felt that way.

"Where do you go?" The sightless eyes sought him without success. "Why do you go?"

"It's time for me to go. I need to be with my family."

"Bring your head close. Let me touch your face. I want to sculpt you before you leave. I am sorry you leave." Tears came in her eyes. She shook her head. "I need you here. It's so lonely."

It seemed a small favor with death coming on. Morgan

lowered his head and felt the small, inquiring fingers touch here and there, delicate as flowers, soft and smelling faintly of clay and urine. Something more than that came. There was a feeling of small, unexpected pain. There was momentary sickness and a small wrenching as if part of his head had been parted from the rest. He did not, in that moment, forget wife and daughter, but in a way, from that time on, he no longer remembered them in the same way.

It was the drug. He knew it was the drug.

When he found himself again, he felt rested and relaxed. He saw that Kelly was using the clay by the bed, the ever-present clay, clever hands already busily working. The head began to take shape.

Morgan was tired. He decided there was no time left to watch.

Morgan went back to his office. The deep pit he'd sought came, and he fell into it.

But it ended.

He came awake when he heard attendants moving about in the ward. He came up from sleep refreshed. He went for coffee and ate a roll. He went back to his office and got out a pill. He didn't feel he needed it, but the old habits were strong. The sheriff would be along sometime, and he wanted to be fortified for that. If death wasn't to be, then the last of life here would be pleasant. He wondered why death had not come. He was puzzled by it, but had no regret. He'd tried. Maybe he'd built up too much tolerance, and no drug could kill him? It seemed possible, if improbable.

The pill tasted bitter. Bile rose within him, and he found he must spit it out, not swallow it.

Outside, through the window, he saw a sheriff's car arrive.

He went to Kelly's cart. She lay there serene and unseeing, but knowing he was there. Waiting.

"You did something," he said to her in a low voice.

She looked at him with sightless eyes. She smiled slightly. "At first I only made the heads. Now I can do things inside some of them. I don't know how. I only know that when I touch someone, I can do this. I tried with Sandra a week before she died, when her mother came here. There was something bright deep there, but the walls were too high when I tried to reach in. Then it got all black inside. I could see she was going to die. I touched other things, but the blackness stayed." Tears came in her eyes. "It made me feel bad that she died, but I didn't know what to do about it."

"You didn't want her to die," he said soothingly.

She nodded. "No. I wanted her to live. I'm learning. Every day I try to learn. With these in here, there's nothing more to learn. They are dark inside and empty, like Sandra." She nodded up at him. "Once before, I reached up inside and touched blackness like Sandra's. I did it on purpose. He died also."

"Oh? Who was that?"

"Dr. Street. He touched me, he touched others, where he shouldn't have touched us. He was sick inside, all light and dark mixed, so I touched him as he was touching me. I touched until it turned dark red. When I see inside a head like that, I have to do something." She smiled, not sorry. "Sometimes I can change them. I changed you. I saw you were sick and unhappy, and I changed you." Her voice held a note of triumph.

He remembered Dr. Street. The man had owned a reputation for sexual bizarreness. He'd died suddenly a year back, been found dead in his room. The autopsy had said aneurysm.

"What exactly do you do inside a head?" he asked, chilled at the idea of it, but not that upset that people had

died. Death was a part of life, of his life. That she could
cause it intrigued more than frightened him.

She looked up at him with blind eyes. "It's like the other
thing I do, the thing of making heads. I don't know. I only
know what to do when I get there. I don't know how or
why. And I also know I must do it. Even after Sandra and
Dr. Street. Something inside my own head says I must do
it."

"Yes," Morgan said. "Yes, I believe that." He leaned
close. The sheriff had entered the ward. "Would you like
for me to come back for you, to take you away from here,
to take you places where you can sculpt many heads, heads
full of light, perhaps even a few full of light and dark, like
Dr. Street?"

"Yes. Oh, yes." She smiled at the sun-filled window. It
was the first time he'd seen her truly excited.

"Wait, then. Tell no one else what you've told me. Wait
for me."

Morgan spent long days in jail. Inside he ate as he'd not
eaten in five years. He painted doors and walls for the
sheriff. He talked learnedly when asked questions by the
sheriff and deputies, trying to make them like him, trying
to be of use.

One night, when a drunk went berserk, he helped quell
him. He was pleasant and cooperative. He knew nothing
about Sandra's death. The lab reports showed nothing
new. Sandra was just dead.

Morgan said nothing about Kelly.

Newspaper reporters came and talked with him. He was
pleasant to them, repeating the same story to them that
he'd told the sheriff. He could see the sheriff watching
him, then smiling at him. Attitudes shifted. The sheriff
came past his cell and talked to him about signing a paper
promising not to sue anyone. Morgan readily agreed.

He spent the time planning and thinking. He knew almost nothing about idiots savants, but knew he would read and find out more soon. He only knew, from books he'd read long before, that they existed; that there were those who could listen to music and play it back; others who could tell you what day of the week any date, past or present, occurred; others who could remember or add or multiply numbers. A gift to replace what retardation had taken?

Perhaps Kelly had the final gift, the gift perhaps for the times. He found that exciting, a new and better thing to daydream on. He no longer wanted revenge. Perhaps that had gone at the same time the drug addiction vanished. Now he wanted change. And he would be to her whatever she needed or wanted—father, mother, brother, or even husband; he would plan for and about her, care for her.

He found himself unexpectedly smiling at himself in mirrors. He'd found a new thing to believe in. Maybe this time he'd perform better. Maybe this time he'd not let it scream and burn and die.

Eighteen days later he was released, the indictment having been dismissed by a judge who'd read the transcript of grand jury testimony and listened to a sheriff who'd testified that Morgan was apparently, from his observations, not a drug addict and not an alcoholic; that he'd at first thought Morgan was, but now did not think so.

Morgan went back to the hospital.

There were ways to do things and ways not to do them. Morgan knew if he vanished with Kelly, there'd be a hue and cry, there'd be a search. That was the way of the system. He found a willing lawyer and filed quiet papers in the court of the same judge who had dismissed the criminal case against him. Morgan worked hard at his job, creating no waves, no controversy. He was offered a permanent appointment and refused it.

He adopted Kelly.

Then they moved on.

Each day he read the news to her. He told her what he could about famous people and powerful governments and about the rich and the deprived. As he read to her, he sometimes wondered whom she'd change and who would die. He supposed it depended more on what she saw than on what he read to her. She seemed bored but tolerant about the reading. He read to her anyway.

They spent that first experimental winter in Washington, and announced a world tour after the critics saw and commented excitedly on Kelly's splendid unexpected work with the heads of the President and his cabinet.

Judicial Discretion

Steinmetz sat red-faced, tie askew, drink in hand, in his large chair behind his littered desk. We'd been drinking some very good, very expensive scotch we'd bought with a tiny bit of the office proceeds from a personal-injury settlement we'd brought off earlier that day. We were feeling self-congratulatory and Steinmetz was recalling his earlier days as judge.

"I hated loudmouths when I was judge, Robak," Steinmetz said. "I hated lawyers who appeared in my court in jeans, who backtalked me after I'd made my decision, who were cocky but unprepared, who lied to their clients, or came in drunk to try a case." He waved his hand. "That sort of thing."

"Who was the meanest lawyer you ever knew?"

"I had several that were bad news, crooks of the worst kind, but I had one special lawyer who practiced mostly divorce law in my court who deserved the death sentence but never got it. But he was fittingly punished." He nodded to himself. Outside it was Bington winter and there was snow on the ground and new snow falling to turn it clean and white again. A good night for scotch and Steinmetz tales.

I'd been around for a while and I'd heard some stories. "Could that have been Allen Hammer?"

He nodded coldly. "I see you listen to gossip, Robak."

"Town legend," I said. "Local lore. He was before my

time here. I've heard he was a tough divorce lawyer. And
I've heard he was trouble."

"He was both. If a girl was good-looking enough he'd do
her free. He had lots of family money. That was part of the
problem for me. He could make any bond. And he was
slick as sleet."

"I see," I said, not seeing.

He poured another inch of Glenlivet over his ice. "Let
me tell you the true story on what happened between me
and Hammer. I was in my first term as judge, green and
tentative. I believed then and believe now that Hammer
dropped his local live-in girl friend into a deep quarry out
in the county."

"I never heard that," I said.

"He never got convicted. Hell, he never got indicted."

"I'll take your word he killed her. Why did he do it?"

"She made the mistake of turning him in after he
mashed her up one night. They fought over a new lady he
was obtaining a divorce for. When Allen went at mashing
he went at it full-bore. He beat his live-in badly enough so
that she lost three teeth and had to have some tricky
surgery done on her nose. She'd been lovely and Allen
Hammer himself was a good-looking man, very macho,
smooth as a rock under a waterfall. When she signed an
information against him she signed her death warrant. He
knew if he was convicted he'd also get disbarred. And to
hunt the female game he was interested in he had to
practice law. He made bond easily and I then think he
waited, biding his time."

"And killed her?" I asked.

"Sure. A month before his trial date she disappeared.
She wasn't at his trial, but the police had found her body
by then. I let the prosecutor say why she wasn't there.
That made Hammer very angry at me personally and was
also a part of his later *pro se* appeal. In the jury trial he got

convicted of battery causing serious bodily injury plus a count of simple assault. The felony was big enough so that I had a lot of leeway, maximum ten years, minimum a misdemeanor fine, if you took into account all the motions Allen had made and which I could have granted if I had a mind to."

"I remember you did send him to prison and that he was later disbarred."

"Yes. I gave him the full ten-year jolt. The day I did it in court was the same day the Krogers across the street from the courthouse caught fire. Were you here in Bington by then?"

I shook my head.

He resumed. "I was in the middle of the sentencing and all of a sudden all you could hear were sirens. The deputy, who was only half watching Hammer, what with him being out on bond, headed for the window and so did everyone else. That left me and Allen Hammer. I watched him and he watched me. He had the coldest eyes I'd ever seen and I felt pretty lonely up there on the bench. He'd never liked me and I'd heard here and there he'd left me on the bench for the trial because he thought I was weak. He'd said openly he was smarter and tougher than I'd ever be." He nodded. "Maybe he was, in retrospect."

"I remember the story vaguely," I said, leading him on.

He ignored me and tilted his glass back. Downstairs I could hear the secretaries getting ready to leave.

"He came smiling up and said, loud enough for me to hear, but not loud enough for anyone else, 'Judge, I'd sure appreciate it if we could get this thing over quickly. I've got things to do, cases to prepare, fish to fry, girls to look after.'

"I didn't say a thing back to him. I banged the gavel a little, but no one heard me. Hammer leaned forward and said, still smiling, 'You know I know where you live, Judge.

I know about your wife and your daughter, your habits. I get hurt, then maybe one day soon they could get hurt. Or even you. So be quick and kind.'

"I nodded down at him and he turned away and went back to his seat, satisfied. When the excitement was over I laid the ten-year jolt into him. He went white and I thought for a moment, even hoped, he was going to have a stroke. Then he recovered and asked about an appeal bond and I set a fat one, but he made it later anyway. He looked back at me when he was on his way out of court and to jail before he made bond and gave me a nasty nod." Steinmetz poured one more inch into his glass, measuring it with a critic's eye.

"So now you had a mean, angry lawyer you were sure had already committed one murder after you?" I asked.

"That's the way of it. When he made bond I packed the wife and daughter off to some relatives in New Jersey for a visit. Her brother was a police lieutenant there and I sent him a photo of Hammer and the information on him just in case. Then I went down to Lou Calberg's clothing store and borrowed a manikin from him. I dressed the manikin in my clothes, the same ones I'd worn the day of sentencing, and put it in the living room in my rocker watching the old black-and-white television. I pulled the shades, but I left one up far enough for a window peeper to see in. I even hooked a very thin wire to the rocker so I could rock it now and then."

I poured two inches of Glenlivet in my glass.

"It took some time. He was a real fox. But it was dark inside. There was only the flickering light of the television. He could see someone he presumed to be me. The fifth night he came on in. He jimmied up a window and came down my hall with a pistol. I waited until he was in the room and had fired two shots into the manikin. It jerked with the first shot and disintegrated with the second and he saw what I'd rigged and I could see him go tense. I stepped out of the closet with a twelve-gauge pointed at him. It was cocked and I think he knew I wanted to give him both barrels. He dropped his pistol and watched me and never said a single word until the police came, just stood there hating me. I'd not only sentenced him to prison, but now I had him again and he knew I'd ruined him. I could almost smell him thinking." Steinmetz nodded. "It was enjoyable. You don't have to give a man bond in an attempted-murder case. I disqualified myself, but another judge ordered him held without bond and it stuck."

"I heard he sued you."

"He did. He claimed he'd been breaking in my house to look for papers which would show I was biased against him and that I'd used illegal deadly force to protect my property, in other words that I'd pulled the first gun. He sued for a million dollars, which was a lot of money then. I enjoyed that, too."

"You got sued for a million and you enjoyed it?" I asked, not sure about his sense of humor.

"Sure. I had the ruined manikin, which Calberg never would let me pay for, I had his pistol with two shots fired and my shotgun with none fired. I had more. What Hammer forgot was that, in a sentencing, everything is recorded. When he thought he had me one on one we had an audience. Everything he said to me at the bench was on the record. Most of his divorce cases weren't recorded and maybe he just forgot. So even with the sirens you could hear him threatening me. I was therefore allowed to be afraid of him and I could use deadly force even if he wasn't armed. They laughed his case out of court and he went to prison for his ten years, came back for another trial on his attempted murder of me, got twenty more and died there.

I used to get cards from him from prison, veiled threat sort of things, but he never made it out to try anything else."

"Well, you could have killed him," I said.

"I didn't want to do that. I wanted him alive. I wanted him in prison looking back at his ruined life and remembering the girl in the quarry for the rest of that life. This is a small town, Robak. I knew that girl in the quarry. Remember I said I borrowed a manikin from Lou Calberg and he'd never let me pay for it? He had a reason. The dead girl was his daughter."

The Profession

We were sitting in the downtown Moose waiting for a land-condemnation jury to arrive at a verdict. Waiting time is always bad time, even when all you're fighting over is how much money a piece of land taken from your client by the state is worth. We were drinking. It was midafternoon-quiet in the old club and we sat in the decrepit but comfortable leather chairs, sipping at bourbon and branch.

Now and then Junior, the bald bartender, would flip open the grub and booze hole and critically inspect the level of our drinks. Outside it was Bington summer, the air laden with flower-and-green-leaf smell, the sun hot enough to burn the unwary. Inside it was winter-cold from the air conditioning.

To fill the time I asked Senator Adams, "When did you decide to become a lawyer?"

He stared around the room. On one wall hung a moose head and on the others there were photos of Kentucky Derby-winning horses interspersed with pictures of long-gone members from twenty to fifty years back, plus a couple of framed royal flushes that proud (or cheating) members had drawn back the years. The senator was old enough to have known the people in the photos and to have seen those optimum hands played out. Maybe he'd bet on the horses, too.

"My father was a lawyer, Robak," he said testily, more interested in his drink and the quiet than my attempt at conversation. Our partnership was fairly new and he was the pro and I the pupil. "He considered it the only true profession," he added.

I nodded, persisting. "I've heard you say that, but I also remember you telling me you didn't get on very well with him when you were growing up and that you wanted to be a doctor or a veterinarian and not a lawyer."

He nodded. "Correct. Your memory's getting better. I wish it would do that well in final arguments. My father was a man who lived to work. I'm sure he was, as I think back on it in my now declining years, a fine man, but I thought he was both authoritarian and overbearing when I was growing up. He was, early in his life, trained for the ministry and he came to Bington as a baptist minister."

"I hadn't heard that."

"I hadn't told you," he said. "Somehow, after he got to Bington, he decided that saving men's souls wasn't for him and so he began to read law nights in old man Kirby's office. I still got my share of personal sermons, but pretty soon he was mostly out of the soul business and into the law business. He took to it the same sort of fervent approach he'd had being a minister. He didn't only try to win cases, he tried to save the souls of the cases he took. He was an advocate's advocate. He liked being a lawyer. And he tried repeatedly to make me like it, but I didn't, not at first."

"Why not?" I asked, now mildly sorry I'd started the conversation. I'd heard some general stories about his father before. They'd become friends only late in his father's life. Sometimes I thought that Senator Adams put up with me better because of his own past history.

He said, "In my seventeenth summer I was crazy about dogs and cats and animals of any kind and I wanted to be a vet, not a medical doctor. Humans could go to hell and I thought most of them would. No one's yet proven me wrong on that."

"Granted," I said.

He gave me a scornful look, as if he knew I was being agreeable to lead him on. "I used to hang around Doc Hagthorpe's place and he'd let me ride with him in his Model T sometimes when he went on calls. He was a man's man, very handsome. When he wasn't out on a sick cow or a horse with spavins he was addicted to stiff shirts and flowery ties and he affected a big gold stickpin. Women liked him, lots of women. When he had something female going, or thought he might, then I didn't ride. But lots of times it was strictly business and I was available and free. He had a wife and a couple of kids, the kids lots younger than me. His wife was beautiful. She had one of those fragile faces which looked younger than mine. She was maybe thirty years old with two towheaded kids trailing after her, but she was kind and gentle and sweet. I was in love with her that year. I hated Doc for running around on her, but there was nothing I could do and he was the only vet for miles around." He nodded. "Then Doc got murdered."

I vaguely remembered hearing something about that in my several years in Bington. Old cases were part of the oral history of the town and the Hagthorpe murder was one I'd heard mentioned, a famous case. But all I remembered was that they'd found Hagthorpe with his head smashed in and that there'd been a scandalous murder trial. I couldn't even remember how it had come out.

"My father defended that one," Senator Adams said. "He'd tried to get me to come to his trials before and I'd never done it, but this time I slipped in and watched some of it. A farmer named Robinson was charged and he was a bad man, cruel to his wife and kids, mean with his neighbors, always gossiping about and challenging the world around him. He drank too much, he didn't pay his bills. He was generally considered a circular, never-ending bastard."

I settled deeper in my chair and that got his attention.

He looked at me and smiled. "He had a reputation any lawyer would envy today."

"Are you saying lawyers enjoy being thought of poorly?"

He nodded. "Of course. Along with the rest of the town I hated him. I knew him a little. Once we'd driven out there for a cow that was down. I guess I felt even more vindictive than the town after Doc's murder. That murder left his beautiful wife alone with young kids. I went past and helped, when she'd let me, but I could see she was devastated, broken mentally and physically. I dreamed, at times that summer, about marrying her and making it all right for her again. Tarzan seventeen, Jane thirty, kids four and five." He smiled, remembering. "I was more idealistic in those days. Now I'm more lawyerly."

I nodded and waited, knowing there was more.

"I'd sneak up in the courtroom balcony where Pop couldn't see me. I wanted badly for him to lose. I wanted Wayne Robinson to get convicted and get electrocuted. I wanted him dead." He nodded and tipped his glass back. "The favorite local story that summer was that Doc had been fooling with Wayne Robinson's wife and that Wayne had found out about it, laid in wait for him near Doc's home, and used a hammer on him. The state had lots of circumstantial evidence. Robinson had threatened Doc a couple of times publicly. A fresh-cleaned hammer was found in his barn, and Robinson was drunk that night and couldn't account for his whereabouts. His clothes were dirty and torn, as if he'd been in a fight. Some witnesses had seen him early in the evening trailing Doc. I sat and watched and was pretty satisfied with everything I saw except the tricks my father kept pulling."

He was under his own spell by now, intoxicated by his own story. When he looked at me all I had to do was nod to keep him going.

"Pop was the orneriest, most cantankerous lawyer I guess there ever was in Bington. Prosecutor Daggett couldn't ask a question without my father being all over him. Everything was incompetent, irrelevant, or immaterial. He was the same way on the exhibits. He objected to the hammer, saying it wasn't the proven murder weapon and hadn't been shown to be related to the case, he objected to Robinson's dirty, torn clothes, and to photos the police had taken at the scene. Old Judge Means was sitting on the bench and he was a stickler for things being right and legal so some of the objections got sustained. Every time that happened you could hear a little sigh go through the courtroom, which was hot and smelly with onlookers, and people would kind of look angrily at each other. Like I say, Robinson was hated. And everyone in the county knew he'd done it."

"I've forgotten how it came out," I said.

He didn't seem to hear me. "But all the objections in the world didn't seem to make any difference in the state's case. They had Robinson and you could see it in the jurors' faces when they'd go out for recesses or when the lawyers were arguing law and they'd get sent to the jury room." He shook his head. "Back then jury trials weren't as civilized as they are now. It was a form of local entertainment to come to them and a lot of the town either came or kept up with what was happening by sending someone to watch for them and report. And it was summer, like now, only in those days it wasn't air-conditioned in the courtroom. It was hot as the doorstep of hell."

"I still don't see how this made you change your mind about being a lawyer," I said.

He held up his hand. "When it got to be Robinson's

defense time Pop called the defendant and asked him
solemnly if he'd killed Doc Hagthorpe."

"No, sir, I never did that," Robinson said. "I didn't like
him, but I sure didn't kill him."

"Did you threaten to kill him?"

"Yes, I did that. I told him I didn't want him around my
place when I wasn't there. I told him if I caught him I'd
take a pitchfork to him."

"But all you did that night was get intoxicated, wander
around the countryside, and then wake up with dirt on
your clothes and with the hammer at your side in your
barn? A clean hammer?"

"Yes. As God's my judge."

"Could you have been in a fight?"

Robinson shook his head. "I was so drunk I don't remember what I did. But I think I'd have remembered killing
someone, not ever having done that before."

"I've heard that song before," I interrupted.

The senator smiled at me and continued. "Pop nodded
and I found myself nodding. It was a reasonable explanation. Of course no one believed Robinson and the prosecutor went after him like a cat after a mouse on cross-examination, but Robinson stayed with his story. Then my father
called Robinson's wife and he asked her about Doc
Hagthorpe's attentions to her and she said he'd been a
friend was all. The prosecutor objected, but Means overruled it. There was some snickering in the courtroom
when that happened. Pop then tried to make it look like
maybe she'd done it, but she said she was at church that
night and there was a whole bunch of people who knew
it." He nodded. "There were, too. The town knew it and
the prosecution knew it, too." He nodded his white head.
"It didn't seem to bother Pop at all. I think he knew it
before he asked her the questions. All he did was leave off
questioning her and call the next witness on his list. He'd

subpoenaed about everyone in town with anything against Doc, plus a lot of husbands and wives whose names had been whispered along with Doc's in town gossip."

"Why didn't he just take statements from all those people?" I asked.

"He tried. Things were different, evidence-wise, then. Some people wouldn't talk to Pop at all. He apparently thought others were lying. He must have run onto problems early so he just waited until up on trial date and started issuing subpoenas as he needed witnesses. You see he believed Robinson. No one else did, but Pop believed well enough for everyone."

The grub hole from the barroom opened and the bartender stuck his hairless head back through. "You ready?" he asked us.

I looked down. My drink had gone dry without me noticing it and I saw the senator's had also. I nodded.

The senator nodded too and then went back to his story.

"Pop kept it up doggedly for three days and I could tell the judge was getting provoked with him and the spectators were even worse. He'd get asked about his next witness and he'd go to a long, two-page list beside him and call one and you could hear a murmur go through the courtroom and the judge would look up at the ceiling and frown. I started feeling sorry for Pop what with most of the people in the county mad at him."

"Well, we both know you can't make any trial last forever," I said.

"Sure, Robak," he said carefully, "but I figured later that what he was doing was setting the scene. There was one apparent witness he didn't call and didn't call until all of us watching decided he'd either forgotten her or knew she had nothing to say."

"Doc Hagthorpe's wife?" I asked.

He nodded and grinned. "You're not as dull as some say you are, Robak. You show minor promise."

"So he called the wife?" I prompted.

"He called her. He'd subpoenaed her early and left her in the hall for three days waiting to testify. There was a separation of witnesses and the judge wasn't letting the witnesses who'd testified talk to those who hadn't. She came in and took the oath and he went after her the same way he had others, mean like, as if he knew something." He nodded to himself. "Only this time he did a little better. Maybe she thought all the people she'd seen going in and out of the courtroom had been testifying about her, maybe she just had a guilty conscience, but he got some good stuff out of her. I can remember him thundering, 'You hated your husband because he was unfaithful to you, didn't you Mrs. Hagthorpe?'

"She said, 'I didn't hate him. I hated him being with other women.' She sat there on the stand, looking like an angel, and I wanted to take a whip to Pop. If he'd been watching me at all for the year before he had to know I was sweet on Doc's wife. Going after the others had been all right, but not my beautiful and sweet Faye Hagthorpe."

"And so you killed him to punish him?" Pop asked her, looking more like the minister he'd been than the lawyer he was, frowning, and looking righteous all at the same time.

She gave him a strange look and the courtroom got dead silent. Even the judge leaned forward. I did too, wanting her to answer right, wanting Robinson dead.

"Not to punish him," she said so soft I had to strain to hear it. She put her head down and looked at the floor, then started crying a whole gusher of tears.

My father stared up at the judge. Jury trials are tenuous, fragile things. I could see his face. He had what he wanted. "No more questions."

There was a sort of uproar in the courtroom and I saw the sheriff and the prosecutor conferring and then saw them go up to the bench along with my father. And, all the time this was happening, poor, lovely Faye Hagthorpe sat in the witness chair as if she was in some kind of hysterical bad dream. I could tell the prosecutor was afraid to ask her anything and maybe make his case worse. He still had Robinson on trial. He still wanted to convict him. Eventually she got excused as a witness and sent on home, with stern orders from the sheriff to stay there.

"I remember now," I said. "The defendant was acquitted."

Senator Adams nodded.

"And that's when you decided you wanted to be a lawyer?"

He shook his head. "Not then. The sheriff got to looking around at the Hagthorpe place after the trial and he found some stuff in Doc Hagthorpe's basement, a bloody sheet, some notes Faye Hagthorpe had found of Doc's from other women and then scribbled things on about how evil he was, plus another hammer which could have done the job. So she got indicted."

"I've never heard of that trial."

"It got venued way up north. Pop took her case. It made the prosecutor mad as hell at him, but it didn't stop my father. He proved all the stuff the state had proved against Robinson in the first trial for a defense, kept Mrs. Hagthorpe off the witness stand, and the jury was only out about an hour and found her not guilty. She left town soon after that. I was temporarily crushed, but, being fickle, I soon found a new love to dream on." The senator smiled. "It was a classic case of there not being sufficient evidence to convict anyone when you looked at the whole body of evidence. So both defendants got off."

"And so you became a lawyer."

He shook his head again. "No. Not because of that. As I said, my father knew I'd mooned about over sweet, probably murdering Mrs. Hagthorpe all that year and realized I'd not liked what I knew Doc was doing. I decided to be a lawyer when I found out I was the last witness on Pop's list, not yet subpoenaed, but with one waiting for me. I was one of the ones he was going after. That's advocacy."

The bartender opened the grub hole. "I just had a call from the bailiff. Your jury is in. Should I hold the drinks?"

The jury could wait a moment. "Bring mine," I said.

"Mine too," Senator Adams said, grinning at me.

On the Rocks

That was the late summer day later remembered at the club as the time five golfers went out for eighteen and only four came back after the first nine holes.

Sheriff Barger was one of the four survivors. He sat at a table in the bar with the other three.

"Now," he said, "I want to know exactly where everyone was when Judge Hinshaw fell into the sharp rocks near the ninth hole?"

The ambulance had come and gone. It had entered the drive of the country club with red lights on and siren screaming, startling the children in the swimming pool, but it had left silently enough. *No need to hurry,* Barger thought.

"I lost my ball farther down the creek," Edwards, the newspaper editor, said. "It's not so steep down there and I saw it and went down for it." He sighed gustily. "I was hooking everything again. When the judge screamed I was trying to dig the ball out with a two iron and wishing I had some contraption like you carry, Sheriff, you know that telescoping thingamajig with a ball retriever on the end." He nodded. "All this and the triple bogie I took on the seventh hole have made me very nervous and thirsty. I'd like to have a drink. Can't we please have a drink now?"

Sheriff Barger relented. He didn't want them drunk and babbling, but he was thirsty himself. "Maybe one drink."

Edwards nodded up at Jan, the brown-eyed girl who

usually tended bar stoically on Wednesdays and Saturdays when the Jug Finders played.

"I'll have a see-through screw, Jan." He smiled. He was a thin man, very devious, the poorest golfer in the group, but one who planned every shot to take maximum advantage of his failings. Because of the hook he drove off tees facing at about twenty degrees away from his hoped for line of flight.

"Make it a double since we're limited to one," Edwards added.

George Dart, the happy dentist, nodded. "Double that double order, Jan." He looked at Sheriff Barger. All the men at the table were in their fifties, sixties, or early seventies and they'd played golf together for a long time. The Jug Finders was a drinking society in addition to being a golfing group. On the course they fought each other for every dollar that went into the communal drinking pot, exultant about good holes, despondent about bad ones.

"How about you, Doc?"

"I was, as usual, in the woods. I'd sliced my second shot, also as usual. I didn't even hear the scream, but I'm getting a trifle hard of hearing."

That was true, Sheriff Barger thought. *Dart could occasionally hear a loud clap of thunder. But he had sharp eyes.*

"Did you see anything?"

"I came out and saw you all standing there and then saw Judge Hinshaw in the rocks." He looked at Barger. "Are you sure he was dead, Sheriff?"

"I'd stake my life on it," the fourth man said. He was a retired lawyer-banker who owned a chain of theaters. He was full of bright, sometimes dry remarks and he'd hated Judge Hinshaw enough to take a series of lessons from the pro to improve his game so as hopefully to beat the judge, Barger remembered. His name was Walter Rose.

"Where were you, Walter?" Barger asked.

Rose nodded at Jan to bring him another drink. He'd evaded Barger's semiorder not to drink by getting a lemonade and then having Jan dump a double of gin into it. He'd claimed he needed it because of his "cough."

"I was in the cart. My second shot was over the creek. After I'd managed that with my trusty three wood I drove dutifully back and rang the bell so the group behind us could tee off. I think I may have heard the poor judge scream, but he'd been screaming and cheating for years and I didn't think much about it." He shrugged. "I didn't even bother to look."

Barger looked up at the pictures on the wall of the bar. There golfers clad in the clothes of their times stood proudly holding cups won for skill on the course. One could look long and far and discover few Jug Finders. They'd ritually be found in the bar bemoaning their luck when such winners' pictures were taken.

"As I recall," Sheriff Barger said to Rose, "you threatened the judge when we were playing the third hole."

"You know what he was doing?" Rose asked intently. "He hit his drive into the pines on the right. When I saw him, he was kicking it out into a good lie where he'd have an open second shot. Then he failed to count at least one shot he had on his adventurous way to the green. I saw him put down a five and he had a six at best."

"We should have made him quit keeping score long ago," Dr. Dart said. "He'd gotten into a new habit of subtracting a stroke from his score on a hole or two. Critical holes."

Edwards nodded. His fingertips were blue from printer's ink and Sheriff Barger thought he remembered seeing a smudge like that on Judge Hinshaw's yellow golf shirt.

"He was a genius with numbers, with misfiguring them, I mean. None of us ever understood how he figured things out and so we let him keep doing it and paid what he announced."

Jan picked that moment to bring the drinks. She handed Barger his lite and set the rest of the drinks on the table. Her voice was soft but firm. "I'll tell you another thing he was doing. He'd come in with you guys and take charge of the money and then he'd pocket some of it. He'd tell you he'd tipped me when he hadn't. All the time he'd be pinching me every time I got in range. I know you guys use all the money you lose to buy drinks, but it wasn't happening that way." She shook her head. "He was the cheapo to end all cheapos."

"Were you here in the clubhouse all afternoon?" Barger asked her.

"No, but I wasn't out on the course or one of you would have surely seen me." Jan gave them her best gamin smile. "I was doing what I was doing, but not with Judge Hinshaw. Dirty old man is what he was."

"All of us are that," Edwards admitted uncomfortably.

Jan smiled cryptically. "There are sexy senior golfers and there are dirty old men. I count you boys in the former group. I counted Judge Hinshaw in the latter." She shook her head firmly. "He made a pass at every woman who was dumb enough to get within 'gimme range.'"

"Makes me glad I'm single," Barger said.

"You're the only one who is. The rest of us and our wives have had to put up with his beastly ways for years," Rose said.

Sheriff Barger made his decision. "It has to have been an accident. If any of us had done it one of the others would have seen it. I was out of sight of him on top of the creek when he went in. Too bad it had to be at that one real bad spot where all the jagged rocks are. It sure tore him up."

"He stole golf balls, too," Dr. Dart mused. "On eight I'm

certain he played my ball instead of his own. He wasn't that way when he started with us, was he?"

"Sort of," Edwards said. "He kept getting worse. Not only had his golf deteriorated, but my wife said he made a very firm pass at her the last time we went off on a golfing weekend."

"So did mine," Dr. Dart said, startled.

"Who's going to tell Mrs. Hinshaw?" Edwards asked.

"She knows," Jan said from behind the bar. "One of the other ladies came in from the course and said Ruth Hinshaw had gone to the funeral home to pick out a casket. She seemed to be taking it quite well. In fact she was described as being in good spirits."

"She should be," Dr. Dart said, sniffing. "He'd been giving her a hard way to go for the last twenty or thirty years." He nodded. "The one thing you can say about his golf game is that he was always very good out of sand traps."

Edwards shook his head. "If they were deep traps he'd yell 'fore' and then throw the ball up with a handful of sand."

"The prosecutor is going to ask questions," Sheriff Barger said, more in explanation than worry. "Even if Judge Hinshaw was retired there's a possibility the prosecutor will want to call the grand jury." He shook his head. "And multiple violations of the rules of golf wouldn't, more's the pity, be a defense to a murder charge if the prosecutor gets his back up."

"You leave that to me," Edwards said. "An accident is an accident. If the prosecutor starts wasting county money on something like this then I'm going to write a few editorials. And this is an election year."

"I'll talk to him also," the sheriff said. "Are we all agreed then? It was an accident? A tragic golfing accident?"

He had a chorus of nods. Even Jan, behind the bar, nodded.

"I suppose it would be unseemly to play back nine?" Rose said, his voice questioning. "I hate to lose the day. One can't count on days like this forever. Soon it ll be fall and then winter." He looked forlorn. "No golf."

"We could take a vote on it," Edwards said. "I'm for finishing the eighteen."

Rose nodded. Dr. Dart hesitated, then nodded also.

Sheriff Barger said, "To the tenth tee then." He watched them as they finished their drinks.

It had gone about as he expected it. Now all he needed to make certain of was that he'd not bent or jammed the telescoping ball retriever when he used it to topple Judge Hinshaw from the bank to the sharp rocks below.

They'd wait a suitable time and then he and Ruth Hinshaw could begin to openly see each other. He'd told her for several years she deserved more than the now deceased judge. And the culminating insult, Hinshaw's death warrant, had come on the sixth hole when Barger had caught Hinshaw trampling the green where Barger's putt must travel for a rare birdie attempt. Barger had missed the putt. There was cheating and there was *cheating*.

Sheriff Barger smiled at Jan and paid her for the drinks.

"It just goes to show," she said. "Cheaters never win."

Barger took his golf cap piously off and shook his head. "Let's not speak ill of the dead."

She leaned toward him, her voice a whisper. "In a few months, when this dies down, I'm going to make a special drink for you gentlemen. We'll call it privately 'Hinshaw on the rocks.'"

The Retiree

In the months following the election in which Judge John Walton was "retired" by the voters, he grew accustomed to having lost, if far from content. There was, of course, less money. He had his retirement pension and that was about all. Most of the money set aside for old age had gone into the doomed fight to save Mary, his deceased wife, from cancer two years back.

Partly to cut expenses and partly because of his quest he moved into the Canning area of the city, called that because once, years back, it had been alive with canning factories. Now the area, close by the river, was a squalid clump of old houses, abandoned factories, and boarded-up stores. It was also the area that "the Butcher" had terrorized.

Walton's apartment was on the second floor of a crumbling brownstone. Living in it was a constant fight against the weather, thieves, and the eternal roaches. But the apartment was large and there was a dry central room for his library of classics. It was also close to a shopping center and the huge magazine store there which stocked out-of-town newspapers.

He grew a beard to protect himself from recognition. It came in thick and gray-white. He found he could pass some people on the street or in a store who'd known him well and not have them recognize him.

Captain Richey visited him in early March, two months plus after Walton's last day in office, four months after he'd

moved. They were thirty-year friends dating back to the
days when Walton had been a tough deputy prosecutor
and Richey an able beat cop.

"This place is the pit of pits," Richey said, looking
around the apartment without admiration. "The neighborhood out there is downright dangerous." He shook his
head sourly. "I felt like loosening my gun when I parked in
front."

Walton smiled. "The apartment's cheap and big and not
that bad, Dee." He and Dee Richey had grown closer as
they grew older. Richey's wife had died at about the same
time as Walton's from the same dread disease. They'd
mourned together and become stronger because of shared
misery. At times they'd also drunk together, usually too
much, but Walton was trying to keep liquor out of the
apartment now, knowing his problem and knowing that
the problem interfered with his quest. So he'd not offered
Richey a drink and they were both becoming uncomfortably aware of it.

"I heard around you had invitations to join law firms.
You could have stayed in your old apartment, taken a
cushy job, sat around, and looked important." Richey
looked at the high stack of newspapers beside Walton's
chair. "Can I guess about what you're doing?"

"If you want."

"You still won't admit that the Gracey kid killed those
oldies and bums around here. That case got you beat last
year, but it didn't cure your stubbornness. So one reason
you moved here was to check out things, get close to the
scene of the crimes." He shook his head regretfully. "All
you had to do in that trial was give that punk the death
penalty he deserved and you'd still be on the bench. The
jury recommended it. When you didn't follow that recom-
mendation the newspapers got on you, said you were soft
and too old, which is a laugh. You're about as soft as an

Arizona cactus and you're not much older than me. But the voters read the papers and remembered them on election day and kicked you out."

"I believed Gracey's story."

"That he came on a fresh body and was only robbing it? Bull and double bull."

Walton nodded. "He was on hard drugs. I thought it could have been the way he said it was. I even thought it was more likely than not that it was that way. He'd never been involved in a violent crime before. And his story checked out on some of the earlier killings. They never did tie him to anything else."

Richey shrugged. "If he was only a druggie he was a very dumb druggie. And you were a very dumb judge for believing him. You couldn't suspend his sentence because it wasn't suspendable, but you gave him the shortest term of years you could. How come, since you sent him to jail, there've been no more mutilation killings?"

"There have been."

Captain Richey shook his head. "None," he said positively.

"Just not here," Walton said. "Maybe soon." He nodded down at the stack of newspapers. "One day now our butcher boy will come home." He nodded surely. "He's restless. He moves around, city to city. I think he could be someone I sentenced, Dee. Or someone I committed to a mental institution or granted judgment against. Someone who had reason to hate me. When he saw what was happening after Gracey was picked up he gave himself a small vacation, maybe to help me lose my job." He sighed. "But there were so many cases down the years. I tried checking them out, going through old files, but there were just too damned many."

Richey shook his head. "You'll put out your eyes reading old files and all those newspapers. There's a lot of misery in the world, a lot of bad, bad people. You sentenced thousands of people, granted judgments against thousands more. You should have given Gracey the death penalty. I couldn't believe it when you didn't. The meanest, toughest judge in the city gives thirty years instead of the death penalty?" He shook his head. "The death penalty would have satisfied the voting mob."

"So I could be judge again? So I could sit on the bench and watch the world go more wrong every day?"

"It's the only world we own and your law is the only answer we have," Richey said defensively.

"For you and for me maybe. But not for those victims out there. How many murders are there a year? Better, how many get away with it? How many do we catch who thereafter get off in court or on appeal? So I was supposed to sentence a kid already half dead from drugs to death to save myself politically?" Walton grinned sarcastically. "In the name of humanity?"

Richey nodded soothingly. "Yes. In the name of humanity. But you didn't so let's forget it all and go out on the town—on me. I'll buy you drinks and a steak. I can see I'm not going to get any drinks here. Maybe a bit of good free bourbon and some red meat will bring you to your senses and tomorrow you'll find one of those firms that offered you a soft job and take it."

Walton smiled. "Booze has never made me sensible yet, but I herewith accept your offer and we have a contract."

"Nothing has ever made you sensible," Richey said darkly. "You are the most single-minded, stubborn man I've ever met." He smiled, changing his whole face. "I can't understand why we get on well."

There were many crimes in other cities which captured Walton's eyes. He carefully clipped each one from the paper and looked daily for follow-up stories. He kept a folder of possibles and probables. When someone was caught and charged with a crime he'd clipped he excised that one from the files.

In Louisville an unknown blade wielder cut the throat and sliced off the nose of an old woman who lived alone. In Indianapolis, a hundred miles north of Louisville, a male in a ski mask attacked an aging night clerk in a fleabag hotel with a hatchet or meat cleaver, killing him, then cutting off his right hand. Mutilation was the key, the trademark for the man Walton's city had called "the Butcher." Usually a hand or arm, but sometimes, in the very old or female, some other, more bizarre part.

In Chicago, the following week, someone set fire to an old alcoholic as he lay sleeping in an alley. Walton listed that one as a maybe. There were a lot of maybes.

Walton's clippings crisscrossed the land, North, West, and South. But not East, not here. Now and then Walton gleaned something for his file from an Eastern newspaper, but nothing he could call a probable. The file grew bulky.

It was someone who had to kill, hated the old, existed to savage and mutilate them. Someone who'd lived at least part of his life in Walton's city and then had decided to roam until the death heat died down. And perhaps, Walton conjectured, someone who personally hated him. There were lots of people who hated him, a legion of them. He'd ruled his court with a heavy hand, scornful of plea bargains, available for trial, raging against a permissive system, handing out tough sentences, screaming at parole authorities. Twice he'd petitioned the legislature for more and tougher prisons without result.

Walton sat in his big chair and remembered the Gracey trial. There'd been demonstrations outside the courthouse, death threats on Gracey. Citizen committees had met. Before Gracey was charged there'd been block watches, stepped up police patrols, cops in drag and dis-

guise walking the dark streets. When Leonard Gracey had
been caught with his hands in a mutilated victim's pocket
and a bloody ax nearby the city had rejoiced and collec-
tively hated Gracey. Three people had been caught trying
to enter Walton's courtroom with guns.

And then Walton, after a short, vindictive trial, had
given Gracey only a thirty-year sentence and publicly
stated he'd have liked it if he'd not had to pass even that
sentence.

They'd mashed Walton the following November. The
voters had chewed him up and spit him out, used up,
discarded. It still enraged him to remember it. He knew
he was right. And even though the system was frail and
fallible he missed his part in it.

It got unseasonably warm in late March and Walton took
to wandering the streets. He carried a heavy cane and
learned to be adept with it. In a leg holster he wore a .32
Derringer with the bone handles removed for slimness.
Richey arranged for the permit for that.

"If you're going to wander the streets down there you'd
better go armed," he said and shook his head as if Walton
were demented.

Walton found some special places. There were derelict
bars by the river, bars where you could buy cheap liquor
for forty cents a shot, wine for a quarter. There were drug
dealers and men who dealt in young women and pretty
boys. There were flophouses where you could stay over-
night for a dollar. There were apartments like Walton's,
places for forgotten men and women or those seeking
forgetfulness.

Walton had the clippings of all the old Canning killings,
times and dates and places. He concentrated his efforts in
the general locality where killings had happened before.
He became a part of the background of the area, a frail old

man who apparently needed his cane to walk, who abused alcohol. And drink he did, carefully at first, less carefully later, yielding to a lifelong desire he'd been able to control as a judge. But every morning, hangover or not, he awoke to do an hour of calisthenics, working until he was sweating well, until his heart pounded against his ribs. Keeping fit, keeping ready.

Twice he was set upon. The first time it was a lone strong-arm robber who shadowed him back to his apartment and then tried to break in only to find Walton waiting, Derringer in hand. Walton was disappointed when the man had no weapon on him—a common robber preying through strength on the elderly.

The second time it was a gang of kids. They had him down and had taken his cane and were rolling him before he realized what they were about. A shot from the .32 dispersed them, but not before Walton took a nasty blow to the head which left him dizzy for days.

Dee Richey visited him again after that one.

"You're going to get yourself killed," he said, shaking his head.

Walton shook his head wryly. "Here I got you a strong-arm robber in the act, one who'd been giving you fits, here I break up one of your Canning kid gangs, put the fear of the Almighty in them, and you think I'll get killed."

Richey held out the case report and tapped it. "I read about the kids here, John. You're fortunate they didn't bash your head all the way in. You're lucky they were twelve- and thirteen-year-olds. There are older gangs in the area. Merciless gangs."

"I'll be all right."

Richey gave him a wise look. "No you won't. My officers report they see you staggering out of wino bars carrying a load which is far too heavy for you. You put the Butcher in prison, believe that. It's a fact. He's there. But someone else out there can and will kill you. Give it up, John. Go back to work you know or retire for good."

"I'm waiting, Dee. I need to do what I'm doing."

"Waiting for what?"

Walton shook his head. "He's coming back, Dee. The Butcher's coming back. It's spring out there. There are birds building nests, the trees are beginning to leaf out. I can almost feel him moving back this way. I know him. He cost me my job and I liked my job for all its problems, so I found out more than anyone else has ever known about him. He's coming back—soon."

"I should sign commitment papers on you," Richey said in disgust.

Five days later Walton was certain he was right.

The first killing was a bag lady who slept, in good weather, on a bench in a small park which overlooked the river. Other people also slept in the same park on other benches, but the old woman, Magda Lupoff, had owned the river-view bench for two years by right of conquest. She was mean and old and crazy and she carried a set of grass shears in her purse. Walton had seen her and knew vaguely who she was.

The Butcher hacked her throat through before she could cry out or get to her grass shears. When she was dead he sliced off both of her ears and planted one in each of her precious bags of possessions.

Walton called Dee Richey. "He's back."

"We think it's maybe a copycat," Richey demurred. "It was a hot night. Other people coveted that bench. We're questioning a lot of people, mostly bums."

"The people out there on the streets say it's him—that he's returned."

"The people out there aren't capable of making rational judgments."

Walton snorted. "Wake up, Dee. Get your people out on the streets. Maybe this time you'll catch him before he kills half a dozen."

The afternoon papers reported the story on an inner page and made no comment about the mutilation.

Walton went out early that night. All night long he wandered the streets, humming a little song as he crept along, using his cane to feel his way through the night. He drank nothing.

The night was uneventful. Walton continued the routine. At the bars he visited he'd buy a glass of wine and hover over it for half an hour, warming it with his hands, spilling it little by little, watching the crowd around him for new faces. There were some. People came and went. People died or moved on. New faces replaced old.

On a morning two days later, when Walton returned to his apartment, he found Dee Richey waiting for him. A police car was in front of the building with a uniformed driver at the wheel.

"Get in," Richey ordered from the rear window.

Walton got in. The uniformed driver put the car in gear and drove.

"We got another dead one. I want to show him to you," Richey said.

They drove to a place Walton recognized, near the bars, near the river. There were patrol cars with flashing red lights. There was a morgue wagon.

The old man lay in an alley. A bottle of cheap wine was near his right hand. His right hand was near his body, but separated from it. He'd been hacked about the head.

"You know him?" Richey asked.

"Hard to tell. I don't recognize him."

"One of our people who was watching said he was standing next to you in a bar by the river last night, that you talked to him."

"I talk to anyone. I talk and I watch. Why are your people watching me?"

"We're not. But we have people out in that area."

"I see," Walton said, not sure whether he was being watched or not.

Richey shook his head and looked down at the body. "He's been dead since about midnight. I thought maybe you might have seen someone follow him out of the bar."

"No." Walton leaned toward the body and shook his head. "Why him and not me?" he asked.

Richey shook his head and asked his own questions. "Why does he cut off men's hands? With women he's playful. He does rouguish little amputations like noses and ears. But with men it's hands. Sometimes he leaves the weapon, sometimes he takes it with him. Why?"

"He left one where you caught the Gracey kid," Walton said dryly.

The next day, for the first time in months, Walton bought no newspapers. There was no need.

At the first bar the next night Walton got himself a prop. He bought a bottle of cheap muscatel and carried it out into the streets with him. He carried it down alleys, spilling a bit here, a bit there, singing a little, staggering some.

Sometime that night he sensed a follower. There was someone behind, someone who lurked in shadows, a bulky person, but careful as an old fox. Once Walton caught a bit of an outline against dim light. The outline was vaguely wrong, too large on the left, too small on the right. That seemed to mean something to Walton, an old story, lost, and try as he would he couldn't remember what it was.

Walton waited down lonely alleys, but no one came. There was only someone out there shadowing him cautiously. He wondered if it might be a cop that Richey had put on him and hoped it wasn't.

At dawn Walton returned home. All day long he stayed awake in high excitement, hoping the follower would try to enter the apartment. But no one came.

At dusk he went back to the same bar, stayed there for a time, and then bought himself a new bottle and staggered out with it. He went down a dark, deserted alley and sat against a wall and went through drinking motions, letting the warm wine trickle into his mouth, then coughing and spitting it out.

There was nothing and then he sensed that there was something. Someone in the shadows.

The man appeared in front of him, looking down at him. Walton looked up, keeping his eyes half closed.

"My bottle," he said to the man defensively. He saw why the figure had seemed wrong. The right arm was gone near the shoulder, but the left seemed strong. The man carried his left hand under a windbreaker. His movements were quick and purposeful.

The man smiled. "I thought I recognized you. Today I went to the courthouse and asked about you. They said you'd moved down here after you got beat. You're Judge Walton. Do you remember me?"

The face was vaguely familiar, but Walton shook his head blearily. He held the wine away from the man as if afraid it would be taken. "My bottle," he said again.

"You committed me years ago," the man said. "My name's George Taine."

Walton searched his memory.

Taine extended his right stump a bit. "They did this to me one night there in the asylum, Judge. I was asleep and a crazy old man you'd also sent there got hold of a fire ax. He took my arm off." He stopped and studied Walton. "Do you remember now? Believe me, I remember you."

Walton nodded. He did remember, but not the way Taine had told it. The way he recalled it Taine had attempted to go over a wall at the mental hospital where they kept the criminally insane and had lost his arm to a shotgun blast when he'd tried to knife a guard who got in the way. After that, Walton remembered, Taine had escaped from the hospital where he'd been sent to 1 _over from the wound. Years ago now and never found, never captured.

Taine's good hand came out of the jacket. The weapon this time was a meat cleaver. It glistened in the dark. Walton raised his cane defensively and Taine took a foot off the end of it contemptuously, the cleaver singing through the night air, its bite as sharp as the keenest knife, the arm aiming it swift and deadly sure.

Walton threw the rest of the cane at Taine. Instinctively the younger man dodged. By that time Walton had the pistol. He fired it hurriedly one time as Taine lunged at him. Taine slipped to the pavement.

Walton went to the man. The .32 slug had only grazed Taine's head and he was breathing. Walton pushed the cleaver away. He raised the Derringer and pointed it at Taine's head. One more shot. He saw that the man's eyes were open.

"Can you do it, Judge?" Taine asked him. "I can do it, but can you?"

Walton felt sweat break out and run down his back. He tried hard to squeeze the trigger.

"Remember. I'll be back," Taine whispered, smiling.

From far away Walton could hear a distant siren. He looked down at Taine. The man would be back. Walton remembered he'd committed him because Taine had killed before, some kind of family thing, his aged father. There'd be hearings. The legal system had a hundred thousand loopholes for crazies. Taine would be recommitted. The state asylums weren't very secure, weren't made for people like Taine. No place was.

Walton found he could not pull the trigger.

There was another way to end it.

Walton waited until the sound of the siren drew near. Then he picked up the cleaver and raised it high, its razor's edge aimed not at Taine's head, but lower, between the elbow and shoulder of the sole remaining arm.

The Decision

By his tenth year on the bench, Judge Cleve Marshall had become a judge's judge. His decisions were sought after all over his area of the state. Bright lawyers filed change-of-venue motions and requested him. Life was interesting and busy. He had never married and now, at forty-three, thought he never would. There had been women, and still were, in and around the small town of Avalon where he'd lived all his life. He maintained an active life-style. He played fair golf and better tennis. But much of his time was spent, black-robed, listening intently to evidence, studying casebooks for precedent, or mulling over knotty decisions.

He wasn't surprised, therefore, when he was chosen to hear the Fielder murder case. He'd read about it in the area papers and wondered if it would fall to him to sit as presiding judge in it. He *was* surprised, however, when prosecutor Hanks and defense attorney Baron announced to him, at an omnibus hearing, that he'd hear it without jury.

"Now hold on, boys," he said. "I know and admire both of you and I've read a bit about the case in the local paper. I can maybe see one of you wanting a nonjury trial, but not both of you."

Lester Baron rose and smiled at him. "Judge, this woman is accused of deliberately poisoning her husband and daughter. My feeling is that a jury would be swayed by the mere fact she's accused, would disregard the flimsiness of the evidence, and would want to punish Alice Fielder because her husband and child are dead. So I'm asking that you alone hear it. My client has agreed."

George Hanks nodded. "The prosecution is willing to go along because the evidence is circumstantial, with inferences arising out of inferences. We think it requires a judicial mind to realize the full perfidy of what Alice Fielder did to her family." He smiled like a half-open knife. He'd always been an effective but vicious prosecutor.

"So be it then," Judge Marshall said. "How long do you foresee it will take to try the matter, gentlemen?"

"A few days. Certainly no more than a week," Baron said. "Much of the evidence could even be stipulated, but won't be because of a circumstance. That circumstance is, of course, a separate page asking for the death penalty. Prosecutor Hanks is also willing to go along because of that possibility. Mrs. Fielder is a very handsome woman. He believes a jury might convict her but not sentence her to death. And he wants the death penalty."

Hanks nodded. "Will you do it, Judge?"

Cleve Marshall folded his hands. "I've never turned down a case, but I want both of you to know I'd like to turn this one down. My difficulty is that I can find no reason in the judicial code of ethics why I should."

They set a June trial date.

"One more thing, Judge," Baron said. "Do you know Alice Fielder?"

"Not to my knowledge. If she grew up around here, I *might* know her. I vaguely knew her deceased husband."

"She was a Linip before she was married," Hanks told him.

"I don't remember the name," Marshall said. "I still might know her, but it doesn't mean anything to me. If I find out anything which might bias me before trial, I'll get out."

Both lawyers nodded, satisfied.

After they'd gone, Judge Marshall read the file. There wasn't much there to satisfy his aroused curiosity. There was the information charging Alice Fielder with killing her husband and daughter. There were some discovery motions from both sides and lists of witnesses, most of them the expected people—the police officers who'd made the original run to the Fielder home after the frantic call from Alice Fielder, doctors who'd examined the bodies, a toxicologist who'd run tests on body fluids, some neighbors.

If the prosecution was correct, Alice Fielder had poisoned her husband and fifteen-year-old daughter. Judge Marshall wondered what kind of monster could do that. Then, in the middle of the file, he came across two police photos of Alice Fielder, one taken front face, the other from the side. She was a most pleasant-looking woman, not yet forty. Her face seemed vaguely familiar to him. He tried to remember why, but nothing came. He got his magnifying glass out of his desk and studied the face, giving particular attention to the eyes. They stared at the camera. He couldn't tell whether they were sorrowful, bewildered, or merely cunning. It still seemed as if somewhere, sometime long ago, he'd seen it—and forgotten it.

Dr. Leybeck was an aging medical-expert boor. Marshall had heard him many times and had once stated, only half in joke, that the man could put a jury to sleep while describing the results of an ax murder. Leybeck was a forensic pathologist much used by the prosecutor.

When the veteran police officer who'd made the run had seen the two victims, he'd called Dr. Leybeck and he had arrived on the scene in the company of the coroner.

"The poison was nicotine, pure nicotine, distilled somehow either from some old pesticides we found in a shed outside the house or from tobacco itself. Edgar Fielder managed a tobacco warehouse and it was the height of the season when it happened. Both victims were found in their bedrooms. The dishes from a table in the dining room had been removed, but traces of the poison were found in the food remaining on two of the dinner plates. The family had eaten some sort of Mexican meal, very hot and spicy. After Sergeant Jones read her Mirandas to her, Mrs. Fielder said it was enchiladas and she had prepared it."

"What effect would nicotine have upon someone who ingested it?" the prosecutor asked.

"A fatal dose could be as little as one drop. It would first stimulate, then depress the cells of peripheral autonomic ganglia, particularly the midbrain, and the spinal cord. Initially, there'd be a burning of the mouth, throat, and stomach, then nausea, tachycardia, elevation of blood pressure, respiratory slowing, coma, and finally death. These symptoms would follow each other with great rapidity. And from my tests, that's how Edgar and Joan Fielder died." The doctor stared out into the warm, crowded courtroom. It was almost full. Murder cases still drew crowds.

"Did you do tests on the plates found in Mrs. Fielder's kitchen?"

"Yes."

"And the results?"

"The food on them was liberally doused with pure nicotine. Enough to kill ten people. I estimated a time of death for each victim about ten to thirty minutes after the drug was ingested."

Lester Baron asked on cross-examination: "You saw nothing in the house to indicate that Mrs. Fielder had prepared some sort of apparatus to distill pure nicotine?"

"No. I didn't look."

After Dr. Leybeck, there came a parade of neighbors
and acquaintances of the Fielders. They testified concerning public quarrels and threats. Close neighbors testified
to the sounds of strife emanating almost constantly from
the Fielder home and to occasional marks they'd seen on
Mrs. Fielder after the battles. Once her arm had been
broken. Once she'd apparently scalded her husband so
severely with hot coffee that he'd been laid up for a week.
The daughter had sometimes come to school with bruises
and lacerations.

The most telling witness for the prosecution was a next-
door neighbor, Janet Robbins. She and Mrs. Fielder were
close.

"She said one day she was going to kill Edgar," Mrs.
Robbins said.

"Did she say it more than once?"

"Oh, yes. Many times—every time they had a fight. He
was always picking on her or the daughter. Joan ran away
several times, but was found and sent back home."

Coworkers at the warehouse testified that Mrs. Fielder
had been in and out of the place many times and that she
and her husband had had arguments there. They attested
to Mrs. Fielder's interest in tobacco and the availability of
raw tobacco leaves in the warehouse. As one coworker
described an attempt she'd made to hit Fielder with a
hammer while at the warehouse, Judge Marshall studied
the woman from the bench.

She seemed calm enough now. She was wearing inex-
pensive clothes and smiled only when her lawyer asked a
telling cross-question. Her features were good, her teeth
perfect. She had apparently been difficult to live with, and
yet it seemed to have been a two-way street she and her
now deceased husband had so tempestuously ridden upon.
He'd hurt her and she'd hurt him in return. The daughter
had probably been dominated and kept in fear by both of

them, but there were questions about that which weren't being asked and that puzzled him.

A teacher had said of her: "She was kind of withdrawn and strange, you know? She was bright enough in some areas, uninterested in others. Her grades ran from F's to A's. She liked science and reading. Until around the time she died, she was like a little girl, though she'd matured physically over the last summer vacation. She didn't take part in any of the extracurricular activities at the school. She read a lot—those dreadful things they write for young adults now. She came to school, she went home. She was a pretty child, but she seemed afraid of boys. Several times she broke down and cried in class. I took her aside and asked her if she was ever beaten at home, but she'd never admit it to me or any of the other teachers, even when she came to school with bruises."

Police sergeant Jones testified about going to the house and finding the two bodies in the bedrooms. When he had arrived, Mrs. Fielder had shown almost no emotion. She'd politely invited him inside the quiet house, saying her husband and daughter had gotten sick after supper and were in bed. She willingly allowed Jones to enter the bedrooms where he'd found the still-warm bodies.

"I read her the Miranda warning and she said she'd fixed the meal. When I asked her other questions, she said she'd like to have a lawyer first so I stopped."

"Did you search the house?"

"Yes, later. That's when we found the poison on the closet shelf in her bedroom, sitting right out in plain sight."

"Did you find anything to indicate that it had been distilled inside the house?"

"There were some old chemistry things down in the basement—you know, bottles and retorts and tubing. One of those kid sets you can buy in a toy store. We analyzed them, but they were clean. I checked the local night school and found out Mrs. Fielder had taken some chemistry courses there, but I don't know if the stuff we found in the basement was hers or her daughter's." He shrugged. "Or her husband's."

A teacher from the night school testified that Mrs. Fielder had taken enough courses to understand how to distill the poison and would be likely to know of its highly toxic nature. Avalon was a tobacco town and workers in the warehouses had suffered chronic, but curable, poisoning, and those poisonings had been reported in the local newspaper.

The prosecution rested.

Defense counsel Baron made the obligatory motion for judgment and Marshall politely overruled it, pointing out that there'd been three people in the Fielder house, that two of them were dead, and that a prima facie case had been established.

"You may begin your evidence," he said.

Baron nodded and went back to the defense table. For a time he and his client held a low-voiced discussion—seemingly amiable until Marshall saw that Baron was becoming red-faced and somewhat angry.

Finally, Baron approached the bench. "Could we break until tomorrow morning? I need to talk with my client concerning her defense."

George Hanks got to his feet. "I'll have to object, Your Honor," he said smoothly. "Mr. Baron and his client have had some months to prepare strategy."

Marshall nodded and looked at his watch. It was almost four. "True, but I'll give Mr. Baron until the morning."

At the courtroom door, Marshall saw Alice Fielder look back at him—calculating him, perhaps. A tiny memory came and again he thought he might barely remember her. There had been a time after his freshman year in college when he'd summered as a lifeguard at the local municipal pool. There had been dozens of girls around that summer, some older than he was, some his age, many younger. He thought he remembered a face like Alice Fielder's somewhere in that lost crowd. He wondered if she'd been one of his "summer girls." It had been a lot of years.

In the morning, a sullen Baron rested without introducing any evidence. The two lawyers made closing argument and Marshall returned the defendant to the dirty, aging county jail while he considered the case.

For days, he sat in his law library, smelling the dampness and decay and rereading his casebooks. He vacillated. Sometimes he was sure Alice Fielder was guilty but at other times he was not. He did know that two people had died and that a third who'd been present had not and that that was strong circumstantial evidence.

On a day in early July he ordered the court back into session. The prosecutor came smiling into the courtroom and the defense counsel arrived scowling. Neither expression lasted long.

"I find," Marshall announced, "after careful consideration, that there is insufficient evidence against the defendant to convict Mrs. Fielder of murder. At times, in considering this case, I have had the feeling that the defendant probably committed the crime, but I have never been able to say to myself, beyond a reasonable doubt, that she committed the double murder of her husband and daughter. Therefore, I now order that she be released from custody."

He nodded down at the deputy who was guarding Alice Fielder. "I'm sure she has personal belongings at the jail. Return her there and allow her to pick them up." He nodded at her. "You're free, Mrs. Fielder. I hope I've done the right thing. I know I've done the legally right thing."

She nodded back at him, not smiling. There were tears in her eyes. It was the first sign of strong emotion he'd observed in her.

He didn't see Alice Fielder for some months after the trial. Lester Baron told him she'd gone off somewhere to escape the publicity. There had been a substantial amount. Marshall had caught the brunt of it, smiling and repeating "Insufficient evidence" until the public interest finally moved on to fresher news.

He encountered her at a restaurant he favored. He'd never seen her there before. She sat at the bar, drinking a tall icy drink, wearing a tailored dress that set off her figure and face far better than the drab apparel she'd worn in the courtroom. Her eyes were as he remembered them, lost and forlorn, and it struck him that, strangely enough, she might be there hoping to speak with him.

"I see you survived my release," she said when he went over to her. "I want to thank you for it." She smiled without humor. "Some in town still think I'm guilty. I'm about to move away; I've given up hope for a normal life here."

He nodded and waited, sensing she wanted to say more.

"Why did you find me innocent?" she asked. "My lawyer was sure you wouldn't when I refused to take the witness stand."

"You had a constitutional right not to testify," Marshall said. "I found you not guilty because I could see another way the deaths could have happened. Your husband could have poisoned the plates and then gotten a poisoned one by mistake, having meant the poison for you and your daughter. You have studied chemistry, so I didn't think you would leave plates with poison on them in the sink until the police came, invite the police officer in, admit you prepared the dinner, and let him enter the bedrooms without objection." He shook his head. "The only thing that puzzled me about the trial is why you yourself didn't say on the witness stand what I'm saying now."

She smiled. "There was a reason. And you have a right to know. I wasn't going to get on the witness stand and tell what happened, not even if I had to die for it, but I'll tell you if you promise you'll tell no one else. I want you to know and understand."

He nodded, his curiosity aroused. Besides, he found himself attracted to her. He knew she couldn't be for him, but he was still attracted. "You were one of my summer girls, weren't you?"

She nodded. "I didn't think you remembered that."

"It took me a while," he admitted.

She looked into her glass, her face somber again.

"He always beat on us. Maybe it was something that went wrong in his childhood. I could take his viciousness to me, but he was also vicious to Joan. I threw that scalding coffee on him when he was beating her, not me. I could take care of myself, she couldn't. I was physically about as strong as he was. Then, when Joan started to grow up, he changed subtly toward her. He patted her and kissed her and she didn't know how to handle that. It got worse. What he did damaged her.

"Joan carried the plates to the table that night. She must have distilled the poison. The chemistry set was hers; I bought it for her one Christmas when she was about twelve. She was very good at things like chemistry and physics. I heard her tinkering with the set in the basement again in the weeks before it happened and I saw evidence down there that she was distilling something. It never occurred to me . . ."

"One never suspects the obvious," Marshall said. "Or the very young."

"Yes." She nodded. "And I wanted it kept like that. I remembered your kindness when you were a lifeguard. You never really saw me that summer, but I saw you. I loved you that summer I was only fourteen and you were eighteen or nineteen. Love's very difficult at that age. Joan's age. I couldn't sit in your court and say that my sexually brutalized daughter had poisoned her father and herself. I doubted I'd be believed anyway, but whether I was believed or not I couldn't make myself do it. I couldn't for her and I couldn't for me. They were both dead and it was over.

"But I want you personally to know before I move on that you made the right decision. If you can keep it secret I'll be very grateful."

"Where will you go?"

"Someplace new."

He smiled at her. "Stay in touch with me."

"All right." She set the unfinished drink down and got up as if to leave. She looked at him and said again, "All right."

Finder

Cannert was northeast of Tampa when the state cop turned flashing lights on him. Instinctively, he looked down and saw he was doing only fifty. He fought panic. Maybe someplace back along the line he'd left something behind, enough for them to trace him. He'd always known that getting caught was a possibility. He pulled over on the berm of the road and waited stoically. He thought about Martha and those he'd come across and disposed of while seeking her. He thought also about the time that was left and hoped he'd not spend it in some jail or prison hospital. The last three nights had been almost sleepless because of the pain. But watching the officer approach his car, he prayed for a little more time.

The state cop leaned in his window. "Man, it's hot on this road, and then I see you driving with your windows down. You got to be crazy."

"Air conditioner's out," Cannert said. It wasn't, but the cold air made him hurt. The warm air did, too, but not as bad.

"Your name Arnold Cannert? You from Chicago?" the state cop asked.

"Yes, sir." Cannert thought of the dynamite in the trunk and hoped the man wouldn't search the car.

"We've been looking for you for days, Mr. Cannert. You're supposed to contact the sheriff at Inland City. Something about your wife and her car."

"I see. Thank you. I've been looking for her for a while.

Do you know anything about her, whether she's okay?
Anything?"

"I'm sorry, but I know nothing more than I've told you.
I'm going to radio in and tell them I found you so that no
one else will be looking for you." The state trooper shook
his head. "It's got to be a hundred out. You better get your
air conditioner fixed, sir."

"I will," Cannert promised.

"Yes," Cannert said positively as they stood in the stor-
age lot, "that's her car."

Sheriff Farmer nodded without meaning. "Me and the
state boys pulled it up out of a deep spot in the lake five
days ago. They got your name by checking out the license
plate. The state man called through to Chicago and someone up there who checked said you'd come down here
looking for her. We got her body in the county morgue.
Another week or so and we'd have buried her. Now you
can take care of that little chore."

"Can I see her body?" Cannert asked.

"Sure. If you want. She don't look good after all that
time in the water."

"Did she drown?"

"I don't know. You ask the people at the morgue. She
was in the car when we drug it up."

The sheriff was a strong, youngish-appearing man with
Indian black hair. He wore the gun on his belt low, like an
old-time gunfighter. He watched Cannert.

A Florida cowboy, Cannert thought. *Mean, too. He don't
give a damn about me or Martha.*

"It might have stayed in there longer," the sheriff continued, "but a fisherman carrying scuba gear hooked onto
it and got curious. He told a state cop, and we come out
together and found her."

The day was hot and muggy. Cannert wiped his face

with a handkerchief. He felt empty inside. A wave of sickness rolled over him.

"You okay?" the sheriff asked stolidly.

"I'll be all right," Cannert said. He got out a stomach tablet and chewed it and watched the sheriff. This man should know about his own area, but Cannert instinctively decided against asking too many questions.

"You sure do look sick."

Cannert nodded. The stomach tablets helped some, but not much. Even the strong pain pills were no longer completely effective. He hurt all of the time.

"I'll make arrangements about her and stick around for a few days," Cannert said.

"Suit yourself," the sheriff replied. "But you look like you ought to check into the local hospital after you visit the morgue."

The morgue was one small room off the side of Inland City's hospital. Cannert found it after driving through the town—a town of maybe six thousand that lay along the northern border of a good-sized lake. It was a flower town, rather pretty, but rather faded in the heat of summer.

The woman in the morgue was his Martha. Her face was puffy and she was bloated and bruised heavily, but it was Martha. Cannert touched her cold, decaying hand gently and nodded at the attendant who'd shown her.

"That's my wife," he said. He fought to keep the room from spinning away from him. For a long time he'd been sure she was dead, but seeing her dead was still bad. The room smelled of formaldehyde.

"What killed her?" he asked.

The attendant rustled through some papers. "It says here she died of multiple abrasions and contusions and shock. Her right arm was broken, and there were some signs she'd been sexually molested. Someone, in other words, raped her and beat her to death." He looked at Cannert. "I'm sorry, Mr. Cannert. I'm just reading what it says here."

"Sure," Cannert said. *And after she was dead, someone dropped her in the lake.*

"Would you like to see the doctor?" the man asked. "There's one on duty in the emergency room."

"No, I'll be okay," Cannert said, knowing he'd never be okay again, not in the little time that was left.

Cannert found a rooming house. The money was almost gone. He was economizing.

Mrs. Tilden owned the place. She was old but still seemingly alert. She rented him a spotless room at a modest, summer price.

"How long will you be with us, Mr. Cannert?" she asked, fanning herself.

"Until I can make some arrangements about my wife. She was found in her car in the lake."

"I read about that in the paper," she said sympathetically. "It's a bad area out in the county around that lake."

"How's that?"

"Drugs," she said, nodding sagely. "Our lake is right in the center of the worst of it. They truck it in, and they fly it up from some of them foreign countries where they cultivate it. They even grow it themselves on some of those backroads farms. And most of them hang around right out in the open in their funny vans and expensive trucks at the Main Bar. Bold as brass."

"Oh?" he responded, interested. "The sheriff told me about finding her in the lake, but I didn't know anything about drugs."

She sniffed. "Why would *he* mention them? He lives in a big house and drives a fine car. I never heard anything about him inheriting money."

"You're saying he might be involved?"

"Not me. I'm not saying anything. He's part Indian. Lots say he's a good-enough sheriff." She shrugged, unwilling to speculate further. "Maybe it was something else out there. Locals say that lake is haunted. When I was a girl growing up here, no one would go close to certain spots in the lake. That was back in prohibition times."

He thought for a moment about that. He found that he didn't believe in ghosts, but did believe in drugs. His stomach churned.

"You look real poorly, Mr. Cannert."

"Just a little tired," he said.

"Let me warm you up some of my homemade vegetable soup. You're so thin I think the summer wind will blow you away."

"Thanks very much for the offer, but I ate something earlier at a drive-in," he lied. Thinking of food made him feel sicker.

Later, after calling Chicago and making arrangements for Martha, and after listening at his door and hearing Mrs. Tilden's snore, he slipped out and checked the box in the back of the Ford, being dead quiet about it. He'd stolen the dynamite and caps at a construction site across the Georgia line. There was almost a full case of the explosive. There were also two empty ten-gallon cans of gasoline. Those should be filled.

He didn't like having been found by the state police. If they'd found him once, he wondered how long it would be before someone, feeding things through a smart computer, would decide to check him out. He'd executed a lot of people while seeking Martha. He knew, no matter how careful he'd been, that there were people who'd seen him in areas where he'd killed. Not much time, one way or the other.

He slipped quietly back into his room and went to bed.

Sleep was elusive no matter what combination of pills he took. He lay in bed and thought about Martha as a young girl, remembered her as she'd been when they'd first met, her brown hair, soft lips. It had been a good marriage. Now it was done.

He lay awake and twisted and turned, plotting against those who'd probably done it. Someone had ravaged her, raped her, then killed her. He felt her pain merge with his own. Someone had pushed the car into deep water. Someone . . .

"Drugs," Mrs. Tilden had said. "The sheriff," she'd implied.

The last doctor had told him the cancer had spread alarmingly and that it wouldn't be long. He thought about ways of doing what needed to be done and hoped there'd be time enough. He'd had the feeling, for days now, that someone was behind him, tracking him, someone faceless, but wearing a uniform.

Finally, with bad dreams, he slept.

In the morning, he visited the local library and read what he could find on drugs. He learned that cocaine was a white bitter crystalline alkaloid obtained from coca leaves, a "social" drug. He saw color pictures of marijuana and read it was the most widely used of the drugs.

When he tired of reading, he went to a nearby restaurant and managed some soup and crackers, choking the mess down, then fighting to make it stay. He drove to two gasoline stations, filling a ten-gallon can at each. Then, making certain he wasn't followed, he drove the Ford to a lonely area down a deserted road ten miles from town. He could smell the lake but not see it from the spot. There, with screwdriver and pliers, he removed the insides of the car doors, lined sticks of dynamite in the hollows this opened, and ran a central wire back from an attached blasting cap to the car trunk. When he'd put everything back together in the car, things looked about as they had before. The Ford looked a little more beat up, but the door sides didn't bulge. It would do. The central wire to the trunk needed only to be attached to an electrical source.

He sat in the car and sweated. He thought about ways to tie the central wire to an electrical outlet. Some he discarded as unlikely, some as too obvious. A diabolical one occurred to him and he smiled. He took a separate wire and hooked it to the left turn-signal light socket, removing the bulb first. He switched on the ignition and flipped the turn signal down for a left turn. By attaching a test kit he kept in the glove compartment, he could see the light in it blink off and on. It ought to work. Once, long ago, he'd used dynamite in a highway construction job he'd held for three years. He hoped he still remembered how to wire it. If not, the loss was small. A chance.

He went to the Main Bar that Mrs. Tilden had mentioned. It was small-town typical and uncrowded in the late afternoon. Behind the bar, an old, bald man in a white apron polished glasses. A few other men, clad in bright shirts and fancy jeans, played boisterous pool at a table in the rear, cursing when they missed shots, laughing triumphantly when they made them. A jukebox played country-western music interminably. The place smelled of mildew and booze and sweat.

Cannert took a seat at the far end of the bar, away from the action, and waited until he was noticed.

"Hot out there," he said to the bartender. "Bring me a Canadian and water in a tall glass."

The bartender got it for him and then waited pointedly to be paid. When Cannert paid him, he retreated to his stack of glasses.

Cannert sipped the drink warily. The first swallows almost made him retch, but then he got past that, and the whiskey warmed and burned his stomach and it got easier.

Outside, two four-wheel-drive king cab pickup trucks stopped. Men got out of them and came boisterously in.

By five in the afternoon, the place was almost full. The crowd was mostly men, but there was a sprinkling of well-painted women. The smell in the room had changed to one of paint and powder—and the sweet smell of what Cannert assumed to be marijuana smoke. Cannert was on his second drink and could feel and see himself perspiring —a cold, clammy feeling. He took out a pain pill and popped it into his mouth while the bartender watched.

"You look like the sun's done got you, old timer," the bartender said.

"Got sick up north. A lung cold I couldn't beat. I'm hoping to get rid of it here where it's hot. The doc says it ain't contagious no more. Up north, a little weed helped when I'd get dizzy with it, but down here I haven't been able to find any."

The bartender smiled. "You're either kidding me or you're brand-new in town. You can buy weed around this area on damn near any streetcorner. Half the guys in this room would sell it to you. It ain't considered a crime in this county. It's kind of protected." He gave Cannert a knowing smile.

"Can you get someone in here to sell me a little? I'd sure appreciate it." The bartender examined Cannert again. "I guess you're harmless enough. You better hope so anyway. Some of these boys is mean. The state cops patrol the highways some, but they stay off our side roads."

"Do they now?" Cannert said, interested.

In a short while, a thin, youngish man without much hair, but deeply tanned by the sun, sidled up to Cannert.

"You want something?"

Cannert nodded and they bargained for a few moments.

Cannert brought out two twenty-dollar bills. The man made them vanish. He handed Cannert a small, plastic-wrapped package. He smiled indolently.

"Anytime, pops."

"I've maybe got something of my own of value I can offer to sell at a bargain," Cannert said, low-voiced.

"I ain't no buyer. I'm a seller," the man said.

"Could you maybe pass the word if I gave you another twenty?" Cannert asked. He got another twenty out, and the man made it disappear like the previous bills.

"What's a plug horse like you got to offer?"

"Two kilos of cocaine, give or take a little."

The marijuana pusher eyed him in total disbelief. "Where would you have gotten something like that?"

"I lived in Chicago before I retired. Other people bought life insurance. I got sick and no one would sell life insurance to me. Then, a year or two back, I got a chance to buy some distressed merchandise from a police lieutenant in Chicago. He was a friend. My deal was that it must not go back on the streets in Chicago and maybe cause us both problems. I promised him I'd put it away for retirement time." Cannert nodded. "Now, I'm retired."

"You don't look like the real article to me," the man said doubtfully.

"Sick. Still sick. That's the main reason I need to sell it."

"Stay in your seat," the man ordered. "I'll pass the word. Lord help you if you're feeding me lies."

Cannert sat quietly in his chair and waited.

In a while another man came. He was fortyish, dressed in jeans and an expensive T-shirt. His nails were manicured, but his eyes were obsidian-hard.

"I'm told you have something to sell."

Cannert nodded.

"Take out your wallet and hand it to me," the man ordered.

Cannert got it out and handed it to the man, who flipped carefully through it.

"Well, you own an Illinois license and it gives your address as Chicago. That part's true at least. Where you keeping the stuff you got for sale?"

"In a safe place," Cannert answered. "We make us a deal on it and I stay with you while someone gets the first little piece of it and tests it. Or I'll bring it all where you tell me."

"What keeps me or us from just taking it and burying you?"

Cannert thought on it. "I didn't tell the other guy everything. There's more where it came from, lots more. And I'm hoping you're a businessman and not a thief."

The man smiled without meaning. "I'm lots of things. So are my associates. We already have our own suppliers. I'd only pay you half what we pay them."

"I'm not greedy. Half might just be fine."

"I'll be in touch. Tell me where I can get hold of you. And I'll set the delivery rules."

"Okay with me." Cannert supplied Mrs. Tilden's phone number. "You can call me there." He waited for a moment. "Could Sheriff Farmer be a part of this?"

The man looked at him with something more than contempt in his eyes. "You wired or something?"

"No. Check me if you want." He waited patiently while he was patted down. "I only want you to tell Sheriff Farmer it's funny I wound up here. He'll know the joke."

The jean-clad man nodded noncommittally. "Maybe he'll laugh if he hears about it. I wouldn't know."

When Cannert got back to Mrs. Tilden's house, it was full dark. He opened the trunk and hid the in-sight wire. He pushed the two cans of gasoline to one side, then pulled the car up close to the house, locked it, and went on in.

He waited. He napped and waited, too excited to sleep. All the next day he waited. Finally, when she became insistent, he let Mrs. Tilden fix him some tomato soup and a toasted-cheese sandwich. He managed, with pills, to hold it down. Once, the phone rang to tell him that Martha had been picked up and would be delivered to the funeral home he'd specified in Chicago. On the first day, that was his only call.

In the privacy of his room and in darkness, he took discarded newspaper and some soiled clothes from his suitcase and made up a small package, trying to make it appear to be what he guessed two kilos of cocaine might look like. He wrapped his package in plastic wrap supplied by Mrs. Tilden.

On the second day, the call came.

"You take the Pike Road south from town," a hard voice advised. "Five miles south you'll see a big mailbox on your right with the name Machen on it."

"Near the lake?" Cannert asked.

"Yeah. Shut up and listen. Turn into the lane past the mailbox and drive back to the big barn. Park your car and get out. Bring the stuff. You don't bring the stuff and you're dead. You try to run and you're dead. There'll be people around. Some of those people are watching you. So start now."

"Okay," Cannert agreed.

He went to his room and got the fake package. In his suitcase there were ten lonely one-ounce gold pieces left, the last of two rolls he'd once owned. He took those also. Additional bait. He kept five and put five where Mrs. Tilden would see them. Five should be enough to bury Martha. He put one of his five in each pocket of his pants and let the other three clink against each other in his shirt pocket.

Outside, he opened the Ford trunk, restored and hooked up the hidden wire, and dropped the package inside. He counted as he did it. He'd only counted to forty when it was completed.

He started the Ford and drove carefully over the route he'd been given. Behind him, as he traveled, he thought he saw a sheriff's car following.

He found the mailbox and drove down a narrow graveled lane to a large barn. When he got to the barn, he did several more things. He found a spot where he could back the trunk of his Ford flush against the side of the barn. When he was against it, he turned the wheels as far as they would go to the right, turned off the motor, took the keys out, and turned down the left turn signal. *Set.* He felt anxious and feverish.

The bartender he'd met at the Main Bar came out of the barn and eyed him curiously. "Why'd you park it like that?"

Cannert touched his shirt pocket and listened to the coins jingle. "I guess maybe I thought it'd help me dicker before I open up."

"Ain't nothing on God's earth going to help you now, pops," the bartender said amiably. He reached behind him and drew a pistol. He patted Cannert down and appropriated the three gold pieces in his shirt pocket, but missed the ones in his pants.

"My wife vanished out here," Cannert said. "They found her car in the lake. Who knows about that?"

The bartender shrugged. "We heard that you was related to her from the sheriff. She came bumbling in here with a flat tire. She saw too much. Feisty woman, and built good for one her age. By the time me and the rest had enough of her, she was dying. So we popped her back in her car, fixed the tire, and dropped her in the lake." He smiled. "The sheriff did that. Buried her deep. Then that damned fisherman who found her told his cousin on the state police first, so we got stuck with her again."

Cannert watched Sheriff Farmer's car drive up. The sheriff got out. Two other men got out of the back seat. One was the man Cannert had talked to about the cocaine in the bar. He smiled at Cannert. He was holding a shotgun loosely.

"He got a gun or anything, Jed?" he asked the bartender.

"Nah. Just an old man with dreams of glory."

"You got stuff for us, old man?" the buyer asked.

Cannert nodded. "In the trunk."

Sheriff Farmer nodded. "We saw you put it there. What else did you put in the trunk?"

The bartender nodded wisely at Sheriff Farmer. "Could be some more gold coins. He had some in his shirt pocket. His shirt was so thin I could see them right through the pocket." He clinked them and moved a step closer to Cannert. "You got more gold in your car?"

Cannert looked around but didn't answer. He took his car keys and raised his arm, as if to throw them. The sheriff caught him in a strong grip and removed the keys from his hand as easily as if he were taking them from a child. He said to the man with the shotgun, "If he moves again, kill him. But let's try to keep him alive until we see his stuff. Maybe he didn't bring it all."

"I brought it," Cannert said. "I was dealing straight." He watched the double eyes of the shotgun.

Cannert could hear other men working in the barn. Four came to the door and watched curiously. A big operation.

The sheriff tossed the keys to the bartender. "Move the car, Jed. Let's open her up and see what we got."

The bartender entered the car and inserted the key. Cannert kept his eyes on the sheriff, but he could hear the key being turned. He braced himself, keeping his face impassive. A faintness came, but he fought it.

The blast and the immense fireball lifted him high in the air. For one final instant, Cannert was still alive, and he could see Martha in the flames. She was young again and so was he and there would be, he hoped in that moment, another time for soft lips and brown hair, another time for them. Sight and sound and pain vanished as he called to her and sought her hand.

About the Author

Joe L. Hensley has written for many magazines, in both the science fiction and mystery fields. He is the author of ten previous novels for the Crime Club, including *Robak's Fire*, *Robak's Cross*, and *Outcasts*, as well as one previous collection of short stories, *Final Doors*. Judge Hensley lives in Madison, Indiana.